Rosie Rushton lives in Moulton, Northamptonshire. She is a school governor of a secondary school and is a licenced Reader in the Church of England. Her hobbies include tracing her family history, travelling the world, being with her grand-children, walking, theatre and all things Indian. In the future she wants to write a TV drama for teenage audiences, visit Kathmandu, write the novel that has been pounding in her brain for years but has never quite got to the keyboard, and learn to slow down and smell the roses.

WHAT A WEEK TO GET REAL

ROSIE RUSHTON

Piccadilly Press · London

First published in Great Britain in 2005
by Piccadilly Press Ltd.,
5 Castle Road, London NW1 8PR
www.piccadillypress.co.uk

A catalogue record for this book is available from the British Library

ISBN: 1 85340 871 9

1 3 5 7 9 10 8 6 4 2

Printed and bound in Great Britain by Bookmarque Ltd
Text design by Louise Millar
Set in Legacy and Chianti
Cover illustration by Sue Hellard
Cover design by Fielding Design

My sincere thanks to Nicole Anderson of Unity College, Northampton, who composed Cleo's song 'Changing My Direction'; and to Sarah Weatherley, Ahlam Yusuf and Emma Tappenden, also of Unity College, for their advice to a geriatric writer about the workings of the teenage mind! Sharron Goode, head teacher extraordinaire, has been a source of inspiration, probably without realising it; and my good friend Cindy Rothwell gave encouragement on those days when everything seemed to be falling apart. I am also indebted to Drs Andrew and Eunice Willis for very many things, which will become apparent as the reader gets into the story! You are all superstars.

MONDAY

7.00 a.m.
Cleo Greenway's bedroom. 6 Kestrel Close, West Green, Dunchester
Feeling sassy

There was one simple reason why Cleo was up and dressed at seven in the morning on the first day of the half-term holiday. Money. With everything that was happening in her new life, she simply had to bin her entire wardrobe and start again. Her parents had made it quite clear that there was no way that they were about to cough up any cash. Her mother had done the 'but darling, you don't need any more clothes' bit, which was rich coming from a woman whose wardrobe resembled the changing rooms at London Fashion Week; and as for her stepfather, he had merely grunted and told her that the world didn't owe her a living, and if she wanted more money she would have to get a job.

'Fine!' she had retorted, glaring at him. 'I'll just run in a few hours' hard labour, along with my GCSE coursework, my singing exam and . . .'

She had paused, certain that he would come to his senses and hand her some cash.

'You do that,' he had replied.

'Roy, be reasonable,' her mother had ventured. 'She is very busy and . . .'

'Not too busy to spend half the weekend at the hairdresser's,' he had said. 'If she wants to spend it, she can earn it. When I was her age . . .'

Cleo hadn't hung around for another episode in Roy's 'kids today don't know they're born' monologue – she had heard it all a thousand times before. Instead, she had done what she always did in a crisis – phoned her mates.

'Saturday girl at the hairdresser's,' Jade had suggested.

'Waitressing at that new café in the park,' Tansy had offered.

'It's obvious!' Holly had insisted. 'Get a job at Olé Outfitters. That way you can get all the cool gear at a discount.'

All of which would have been fine except that Cleo got the same answer everywhere she went. 'We don't take anyone under sixteen. Company policy. Come back next year.'

In the end she had been forced to take the only job going in Dunchester for a fifteen-year-old. It wasn't cool, it paid a pittance and it didn't offer any perks, but it was better than nothing and the hours were short. There was just one problem. She would have to tell them that she couldn't work on Wednesday. They wouldn't like it but there was nothing she could do about it.

So much, she reflected, had happened since Jade's disastrous birthday party a couple of months ago. To be honest, when Angus, the totally drop-dead gorgeous guy who ran the KickAss disco with his mate Kyle Woodward, had heard her singing along to the hits and asked her to do a slot with his college band, she'd thought it was just a chat-up line. Sadly, she had soon discovered that Angus didn't do chat-up – well, not with the likes of her, anyway. But she'd gone along with it, just for a laugh – not that the venue for her debut was quite as hip as she'd imagined.

'My mum's on the committee for the League of Friends at the hospital,' Angus had told her apologetically. 'She's roped the band into playing at their Snow Ball – just a half-hour slot in the staff canteen, but it's a start.' He had coughed nervously. 'So are you up for it? I mean, if you're not already doing something . . .'

Like I've got half a dozen guys fighting over my one free evening, she'd thought wryly.

'No, I'm free,' she'd said in the next breath. 'What do you want me to sing?'

'How about "Don't Leave Me Lonely" for starters? Great for your voice and there's the drum solo for me to show off! And Cleo, it's really cool that you're doing this. Thanks a lot.' He had sounded like he really meant it.

That's how it had started. And finished, thanks to her parents.

'Absolutely not,' her mum had declared the day after the Snow Ball, when Cleo had mentioned that the band were lining up a few gigs at Stomping Sam's. 'A charity ball is one thing; cavorting in some sleazy nightclub is quite another. This is a very important year, Cleo. You're taking three GCSEs a year early, you've got your coursework to finish, a singing exam coming up . . .'

'So, like, practising singing would be a good idea, yes?' Got you, she'd thought. Sadly, she wasn't dealing with a normal human being.

'There's singing and singing,' her mother had said. 'And smoke-filled nightclubs won't do your vocal cords any good. It's not that I'm trying to spoil your fun.'

'No, just my whole life, more like,' Cleo had stormed.

'And what am I supposed to tell the band? Mummy won't let me come?'

'Sure.' Her mother had smiled. 'Blame me if it helps. Everyone else does.'

Of course, when it came to it, Cleo hadn't told it like it was; she didn't want to appear a total downtrodden wimp in front of the guys. She'd simply said that she'd forgotten it was her gran's birthday (which was true) and there was a huge family party (which wasn't true) and she'd have to go, boring, boring.

'Families,' Angus had drawled down the phone. 'Tell me about it. Don't worry, there'll be other times. I'm not letting a girl like you slip through my fingers.'

If it had been any other guy, she thought now, scooping up her honey-blond hair into a ponytail, she would have thought he was coming on to her big time.

She sighed, pulled her fleece over her head and ran downstairs, almost colliding with her stepfather, who was wearing his ancient tartan dressing gown and his usual grumpy expression, and balancing two mugs of tea on a tray.

'What are you doing today?' he asked, stopping on the third stair and blocking Cleo's path.

'Going to work,' she retorted. The phrase made the job sound a lot more important than it was, and she liked the way it rolled off her tongue.

'After that?'

'Meeting up with Holly,' Cleo replied, trying to push past him.

'Where are you meeting her?' Roy asked.

'What's with all the questions?' Cleo demanded.

Roy shrugged. 'Just trying to show an interest,' he muttered.

Cleo sighed. She guessed her mum had had a quiet word with Grumpy Guts and told him to be friendlier. This was clearly his best effort.

'I'm going round to her house,' she said. 'She's moving and I said I'd help sort out her stuff.'

'That's OK, then. You do that,' Roy said, venturing the half-hearted grimace that was his closest attempt at a smile. 'That'll be fine.'

As if I needed your permission, Cleo thought savagely, but said nothing. It was always best to let parents think they had the upper hand.

7.20 a.m.
The Cedars, Weston Way, West Green, Dunchester. Parent in overdrive – so what's new?

'Holly! Up! Now!'

Holly's duvet was wrenched from her prone body and a blast of cold air hit her feet.

'Mum, what the hell?' she gasped, grabbing the corner of the disappearing duvet and glaring up at her mother.

'I want you up and dressed in fifteen minutes,' her mother replied briskly, pulling back the curtains.

'Mum!' Holly protested. 'It's half-term, remember?'

She was well aware that her mother had reached the age when she struggled to remember where she'd parked the car, never mind the finer details of the school calendar.

'I can't help that,' her mum blustered, running her fingers through her grey hair. 'The Walkers will be

5

round in half an hour and if they see this mess . . .'

'What walkers?' Holly yawned, giving up all efforts at deflecting her mother and propping herself up on her elbow.

'Oh, Holly. For goodness' sake, use your brain!' her mother erupted. 'They're the people who are buying our house – they're coming round to measure for curtains.'

'What, at this hour?' Holly gasped. 'Can't they come later?'

'They work,' her mother replied abruptly, picking up a mug from Holly's dressing table and sniffing it in disgust. 'I know it's not the best time, but I've got to keep on the right side of them – we're due to exchange contracts on the sale on Friday.' She glanced round Holly's bedroom. 'Mind you, if they see this mess they'll probably change their minds!'

She kicked a pile of Holly's *Heaven Sent* magazines under the bed, and flung a couple of pairs of shoes into the bottom of her wardrobe.

'Well, if mess is going to make them back out,' Holly retorted, 'I'll hurl a few more things about the place. Anything to stop us moving to Ecton Hall.'

'Oh, Holly. Why do you have to make such heavy weather of everything?' Her mother sighed. 'It's a lovely apartment in a beautiful old manor house. It's got that fantastic Smallbone kitchen, a proper power shower . . .'

'And it's stuck in the middle of nowhere!' Holly burst out. 'Why did you have to go and choose somewhere miles away from all my friends?'

Since my friends are the only part of my life that is halfway decent at the moment, she added silently.

'You talk as if we're emigrating to Australia,' her mother teased, picking up Holly's overflowing wastepaper basket and eyeing it with distaste. 'We'll only be five miles away and you'll see them every day at school. Now, get out of bed at once, and get this room cleared up and looking vaguely habitable. Now!'

'OK,' Holly said. 'I can't see it matters. If these Walker people are prepared to pay for this old heap, they're hardly likely to worry about a bit of mess in my bedroom.'

'This house is not an old heap,' her mother replied with a faint smile. 'It's a Victorian house of great charm, remember?'

Despite herself, Holly couldn't help smiling. They both knew that The Cedars boasted windows that rattled in the wind, a boiler with a mind of its own and a kitchen that wouldn't have been out of place in one of those *How We Lived Before the War* programmes, but once Rodhouse and Grundy, the local estate agents, had got their hands on it, it became 'a late-Victorian property of character and charm rarely available in this sought-after area'.

'I hope there's some hot water,' Holly said, sighing. 'I've got to wash my hair before Cleo comes.'

'Cleo?' her mother repeated. 'Coming here?'

'Yes, Mum,' Holly replied patiently. 'I told you.'

She wasn't sure that she had, but her mother hated to think she was losing the plot and always pretended to remember.

'Well, you'll have to cancel,' her mother protested. 'I've got the removal men coming to give an estimate at twelve noon, there are boxes everywhere, your father's taking the day off to sort the attic, and to cap it all, there's this historical society dinner on Wednesday and I've nothing to wear.'

'All of which has nothing to do with me,' Holly cut in emphatically. 'You wanted me to sort my room; Cleo's going to help.'

'Really?' Her mum didn't sound convinced. 'I know your idea of sorting. You'll move two items into a box and then spend an hour trying out make-up and talking about boys.'

She made it sound as if her daughter was intending to experiment with illegal substances. But then, thought Holly, her mother wore lipstick only at Christmas or on her wedding anniversary and even that was the wrong shade for her complexion. As for discussing boys, what was there to talk about? With a love life as dire as mine, she thought, there's nothing to say. But at least Cleo was in the same boat. There was nothing worse than being with mates like Tansy and Andy who went around glued at the hip.

'Besides, haven't you got a whole heap of coursework to finish?' her mother asked, eyeing the pile of school-books in the corner of the bedroom. 'You know what your form tutor said about . . .'

'I'll do it,' Holly cut in. 'I've got all week.'

'And don't just concentrate on your art and English,' her mother added. 'I know they are your favourite subjects, but, let's face it, it's maths and science you need to work at.'

'I know, I know,' Holly muttered. Like working at them is going to make any difference. When will someone get the message that I can't do it any more? she thought.

'Cleo said she'd help me understand my maths,' Holly lied. 'I thought you'd be pleased.'

'Very well, but don't expect me to feed you both,' Mrs Vine concluded, sweeping a couple of empty coffee cups from Holly's bedside table. 'I haven't got time.'

'Don't worry, we'll pick something up at the mall,' Holly assured her.

'The mall?' her mother queried. 'I thought you said you'd be clearing your room and working.'

Holly sighed. 'And how long can that take?'

'Looking around me, I'd say about three days,' declared her mother. 'Now, get dressed. And wear something decent. I don't want you slouching around in torn jeans when the Walkers get here.'

8.15 a.m.
Cattle Hill. Delaying tactics

'Stick thin? So yesterday! Curvy is cool on the catwalk!'

'Now, curvy is one shape I *can* do,' Cleo murmured to herself as she perched on a wall at the corner of Cattle Hill and scanned the fashion section of her favourite tabloid. It was strictly against Mrs Patel's rules for papers to be opened before they were pushed through letterboxes but on Mondays, Cleo couldn't resist sneaking a look at 'Ten Top Tips for Trendsetting Teens'. She'd never thought of herself as a trendsetter – not till that amazing party at Jade's house. Even now, pulling up the hood of her fleece against the faint February drizzle, she could see the expressions of pure amazement on the faces of her mates as she had strutted her stuff to the beat of BagHandlers' latest hit. She couldn't blame them for having been gobsmacked; she had been pretty stunned herself.

'Now I've changed, directions rearranged, so goodbye to that old li-eye-ife!'

She hitched the bag over her shoulder and sashayed up the road, trying out the lyrics to the song she was writing for her GCSE music. Well, not for that at all, really; for the band to use one day when she had the courage to admit to wanting to be a singer-songwriter. Her mother was currently going through the 'don't make entertainment your life, dear; they will only discard you like they discarded me' stage. But studying for GCSE music was the greatest cover-up; whenever her mum burst into her room unannounced and found her singing or playing rock tracks, she simply said it was revision. The fact that her mother actually believed her showed how totally clueless she had become.

She stuffed a copy of the *Financial Times* through the letterbox of a house absurdly called Mee-an-You, and glanced at her watch. Only four more houses left to do and she could go home. The trouble was her mum would be there. There had been a time when Cleo would have liked the fact that her mum wasn't dashing off to rehearsals for a play, or filming for some deadly embarrassing TV advert but right now she would have given anything for an empty house and no intrusive questions.

'Any work, Mum?' she would ask every few days.

'As if,' her mother would reply, avoiding Cleo's gaze. 'You'd think I'd suddenly turned invisible. I'm over the hill, Cleo, past it, washed up. There was a time when the name Diana Greenway was on everyone's lips.'

And she would embark on a long retrospective of her career, or rush upstairs to unearth her boxes of theatre programmes and newspaper reviews.

Lately it had got worse. Her mum seemed to swing from the most amazing highs during which she would telephone her agent and every producer she had ever met and tell them she was just what they needed for their latest production. On other occasions, she would mope around the house, not even bothering to put on any make-up, which for a woman who used to spend hours in front of the mirror was even more of a worry. The arguments were always about the same things: money and her mum refusing to get what Roy called a normal job, like a school secretary or a receptionist at the doctor's surgery, instead of acknowledging that she was a has-been in the world of acting.

She pulled the final newspaper out of the bag and glanced at the number scrawled in the top corner. Number 3 – Tansy's house. She grinned to herself. She was in luck.

'Cleo, dear. What a surprise!' Tansy's mum, Clarity, opened the door to Cleo's persistent knocking. 'Don't tell me you're doing a paper round these days? How enterprising! Does it pay well?'

'No,' said Cleo with a laugh, 'but it's better than nothing.'

From somewhere inside the house, a clock struck the hour.

'I must dash,' Clarity said, grabbing an ancient waxed jacket off the peg by the front door and shoving her arms into the sleeves. 'Trudie and I have got the contract for the new scented garden for the blind in Beckets Park and I'm off to Wisley to source some roses!'

'Lovely,' murmured Cleo. Tansy's mum was a landscape gardener and could get excited about the most extraordinary things.

'Tell you what,' Clarity exclaimed, flicking up the latch on the front door. 'Why don't you save me a job and beetle off upstairs and kick Tansy out of bed? Oh, and try to cheer her up, Cleo – there's a love. She spent yesterday evening moping around the house like a wet Wednesday in Wigan.'

'Why? What's the matter?' Cleo began, but Clarity had clambered into her dilapidated van, slamming the driver's door closed behind her. There was a grating noise, and a couple of explosions as the van backfired, then jolted off down the hill.

Cleo bounded up the stairs two at a time, nearly concussing herself on a huge wooden cowbell hanging from one of the old cottage beams. 'Tansy!' Rubbing her head with one hand, she thumped on her friend's bedroom door. 'It's me, Cleo – can I come in?'

The only reply was a long muffled groan.

'Oh, good, you're awake!' Cleo burst into the room and yanked at the heap of rumpled bedclothes.

'Cleo, for God's sake!' Tansy, tousle-haired and red-eyed, emerged from under the duvet. 'What the hell do you think you're doing? Do you make a habit of bursting into people's bedrooms uninvited?'

For an instant Cleo was speechless. Of all her friends, Tansy was the least like to go off on one, especially over nothing at all.

'Your mum said I could,' she began. Then she spotted a few crumpled tissues on the floor by the bed and the faint mascara smudge on the pillow.

'Hey, have you been crying?' she asked gently, perching on the end of the bed and leaning towards Tansy. 'What's wrong? Is it your dad?'

It occurred to Cleo that ever since Tansy's birth father had turned up a couple of months before and basically told Tansy he didn't want to know her, she had been much more subdued and silent than she used to be.

'No way,' Tansy retorted, sitting up in bed and bunching her knees under her chin. 'As far as I'm concerned, all that is over and done with.'

'Right,' Cleo murmured. 'So if it's not him, what is it? Do you want to talk about it?'

'No,' said Tansy. 'Yes. No. Oh, I don't know.'

'Well, if you want to, I'm here,' Cleo said. 'In the meantime, there's something I need to talk to you about.'

'Hang on!' Tansy said, opening the bedroom door. 'Before you start, I need a sugar fix. There's a bag of mini doughnuts downstairs – want one?'

Cleo grinned. 'Why not? Chunky is supposed to be the new slim, after all. Let's go for it.'

She was relieved to see a flicker of a smile cross Tansy's lips. It didn't linger, but at least it was a start.

Holly flung open the back door, letting a blast of ice-cold air into the kitchen.

'Dad!' she yelled, shivering as she stepped gingerly out on to the patio. 'Where are you? You're wanted.'

'He's round the side of the house talking drains with my dad.'

Holly jumped and wheeled round. A tall guy with jet-black, spiked hair, slate-grey eyes and scrum-half shoulders was lolling against the wall of the house, Naseby held tightly in his arms purring like a badly serviced central heating system.

Her mouth dropped open in amazement. 'Oh my God!' she gasped, 'It's you!'

'Hey, I know you,' the guy said at the same instant, his breath rising in wispy puffs. 'We met at Jade's.'

'It's Angus, right?' Holly interjected, sighing inwardly at the memory of Jade's disastrous party – the time when gatecrashers had totally wrecked the evening and Kyle, Angus's best mate, had wrecked Holly's heart.

'And you're Polly . . .'

'Holly,' corrected Holly.

'I had no idea you lived here,' Angus said, dumping a wriggling Naseby on to the patio and brushing hairs off his leather jacket. 'Cute cat.'

'And I had no idea you were buying our house,' Holly replied. 'Come inside – it's freezing out here.'

Before she could turn round, the upstairs window was flung open and Mrs Walker's head poked out. 'Angus dear, I know you make chatting up girls into an art form but could you please give me a break? Some of us have to get to work and I need you to talk shelving. And where's your father? Honestly, that man is never around when you need him. Now come!' The window slammed shut.

Angus coloured and raised an eyebrow. 'Sorry about that,' he muttered.

'That?' Holly smiled 'Compared to my mother in verbal overdrive, that was nothing. I'll get your father; you go and play the dutiful son, OK?'

Ten minutes later . . .
More and more bemused

'So you two know one another?' Angus's mother remarked after ten minutes of quizzing her son on roller blinds, drum kits and the advantages of spotlights over uplighters. 'How come?'

'He knows every girl in town, I guess,' his father blurted out, slapping his son on the back. 'Right, Angus – eh? Eh?'

'Holly is a mate of Cleo's,' Angus muttered, colouring up and edging away from him.

'Dear me,' his mother cut in with a smile. 'You know, he can't speak for more than five minutes without mentioning that girl's name. It's Cleo this, Cleo that. Just like his father – can't resist a pretty face.'

His father chortled and looked smug.

'Such a dear girl,' Mrs Walker babbled on. 'We met her at the Snow Ball – lovely voice she has, and, of course, if things work out this week, we'll be seeing a lot . . .'

'Mum,' retorted Angus, his face turning redder by the second. 'Stuff it.'

I don't believe I am hearing this, Holly thought. She talks as if Cleo and Angus are virtually an item but that doesn't stack up – not after what Jade told me. But then again Jade isn't always right, even if she likes to think she is.

'Oh dear, I'm embarrassing him again.' His mother laughed, nudging Holly's mum in the ribs. 'I'll say no more. My lips are sealed.'

'That'll be the day,' Angus muttered under his breath.

8.20 a.m.
53 Lime Avenue, Oak Hill, Dunchester.
First aid – but for whom?

'In the case of severe bleeding, a torniquet should be applied . . .'

Jade Williams leaned against her pillow, covered the text in her First Aid for Cadets handbook with one hand, closed her eyes and tried to remember the procedure. She hadn't planned to be awake this early on the first day of the holidays, but with her little cousin Helen practising on her new trumpet in the sitting room, and Josh revving up his battered motorbike on the front drive, sleep was out of the question. At least it gave her the chance to cram; her St John Ambulance test was only a couple of weeks away, and if she passed, she'd be upgraded and actually allowed to do some hands-on nursing.

Well, not nursing exactly – but at least she'd be allowed to go with the rest of the St John Ambulance crew to fun runs and fêtes, and if she played her cards right she just might get to clean up the odd cut or revive a fainting spectator.

'But why would you *want* to?' her cousin Allegra had asked her the night before, when Jade insisted on watching *Emergency Call 999*. 'All that blood and gore – and besides, you're hardly likely to pull a fit guy dressed in that uniform they gave you!'

'You never know,' Jade had said, smiling. 'I might give the kiss of life to a six-foot hunk who then falls madly in love with me.'

It had raised a laugh from Allegra and made Jade sound like the rest of her mates. Which good, because the one thing Jade was certain of – along with her ambition to be a nurse in Africa and to walk on the Great Wall of China – was that there was something really wrong with her.

For the last three months, ever since she dumped Scott Hamill (who was now going out with Allegra – or rather being dragged round by Allegra), she had been trying to fall in love. Every time she decided to make a real effort and accept an invitation to the movies or someone's party, nothing happened. Or rather, what happened was that the guy would grab her hand and ten minutes later, put an arm (sometimes quite smelly) round her neck and then lunge forward in hopes of a kiss. Normal girls, she thought with a sigh, would go for it, but she couldn't.

The whole thing made her feel slightly sick. And considering that all her mates could snog for England, that proved that she was the abnormal one. If only her mum was around, she could have talked to her about it.

But her parents were both dead, killed two years ago almost to the day by a joyrider in a stolen car.

She shook herself and forced her mind to concentrate on something else. The closer it got to Thursday, the anniversary of their death, the more she found herself aching inside. People had told her that time was a great healer but she reckoned that was rubbish. If anything it got worse the older she got, because there was so much she didn't understand about life and herself and there was no one to confide in. Her aunt and uncle were great guys, but somehow Jade didn't feel she could open up to them – not when they had three kids of their own to worry about. There was her gran, of course: Jade loved her to bits, but how could someone of seventy-three possibly understand what it was like to be fifteen?

She slammed her book shut. Not being besotted with boys wasn't the only thing that made her friends raise the odd eyebrow. Jade dreaded a whole week of half-term holiday.

'You are seriously weird,' Holly had told her affectionately the previous Friday, when Jade had complained that half-term was a waste of time. 'No school, long lie-ins, all the TV we can watch – and Rock Hard on Saturday!'

Jade hadn't meant to groan out loud, but the thought of a spending the evening at the Riverside Centre bopping about to a whole load of bands was the biggest turn-off ever. It was the hippest event in the whole of Dunchester Arts Week, and everyone seemed to be really fired up about it. Everyone except her, that was. It wasn't as if she had a guy to hang out with – not that she wanted a guy, but all her mates would either be with someone or out to pull and she'd feel, as usual, like a total dweeb.

'You're up for it, aren't you?' Holly had asked. 'It'll be so cool – there are going to be six different bands, and a disco half way through and fireworks at the end and . . .'

'Great,' Jade had cut in, trying to look enthusiastic. 'Just great.'

If I go, she thought, I'll hate every minute of it and if I don't go my mates will think I'm a party pooper.

She picked up her book and flicked through the pages to the chapter headed 'Objects: Swallowed and Ingested'. Learning how to deal with a choking toddler was a whole heap easier than sorting out her life.

8.25 a.m.
Tansy's kitchen.

'So, what are you doing tonight?' Cleo asked Tansy, as she licked sugar off her fingers and surveyed the last remaining doughnut. 'Aside from snogging Andy senseless, that is!'

'Oh, very funny,' Tansy snapped, jumping up from the table. She eyed Cleo closely. 'He hasn't said something to you, has he? About him and me.'

'Hey, what's up?' Cleo gasped. 'Have you two had a falling out?'

'Sort of.' Tansy smiled. 'Well, no. Yes. Oh, I don't know.'

'So what's the problem?' Cleo queried, wondering if grabbing the last doughnut would be hugely tactless at a moment like this.

'You know he was off school on Thursday and Friday?'

Tansy began. 'Well, I phoned him each evening to see how he was, and he hardly said a word. Normally we chat for hours.'

Cleo shrugged. 'You know what guys are like when they're ill,' she reasoned. 'They get a cold and act like it's double pneumonia.'

'That's what I thought at first,' Tansy admitted. 'But yesterday I called him to talk about going to see a film today like we'd planned, and he said he'd got loads to do and couldn't make it.'

Cleo sighed. 'Do you reckon the parents have been giving him a hard time? You know – the usual bit about GCSEs and work coming before pleasure and all that stuff? My lot never shut up about it.'

Tansy shook her head. 'Come on, Cleo, you know Andy – he'd get straight As even if he never opened a textbook. Besides, his mum is so laid back she's horizontal. Do you want to share this last doughnut?'

'I thought you'd never ask,' Cleo said, grinning. She ripped it in half and shoved the smaller of the two pieces on to Tansy's plate.

'You don't think he's found someone else?' Tansy muttered. 'Serve me right if he has, I guess.'

'And how do you work that one out?'

'Well, I did kind of ignore him a lot back in January – you know, with all the business over my dad. He was really upset.'

'There's only one way to find out,' Cleo told her firmly. 'Ask him.'

'You don't think I've tried that?' retorted Tansy. 'He said he'd call me later, but he never did. He doesn't reply to my text messages and last evening when I phoned their landline all I got was the answerphone. Even his parents didn't pick up.'

'So go round and confront him,' Cleo countered. 'You've nothing to lose.'

'And what if he *has* got someone else? You think I'm going to give him the satisfaction of seeing me grovel? Get real!'

Cleo burst out laughing. 'That's more like you! What you need is a really good excuse to – oh my God! I've got it! I've got it!'

'Got what?' asked Tansy, wetting her finger and dabbing up the last of the sugar from her plate.

'The perfect way for you to suss out what's going on with Andy,' declared Cleo. 'Paper round. Mrs Patel's looking for another papergirl and was . . .'

'Stop right there!' Tansy burst out. 'No way – that is so not my kind of thing.''Will you just listen?' Cleo urged. 'Andy lives in Ridings Way, right?

Tansy nodded. 'And that's one of the streets I'm doing on my paper round. So this is what we do. We tell Mrs Patel that you want to be a papergirl.'

'Cleo, for the last time . . .'

'We pretend, silly,' Cleo said. 'You get to come round with me for a couple of days, supposedly learning what to do . . .'

'Like there's an art to stuffing newspapers into letterboxes?'

'Look, do you want my help or don't you?' Cleo demanded. 'Do you know how I got to see you this morning so early? By knocking on the door and handing your mum her magazines and saying I didn't want to tear them by ramming them through the letterbox.'

'What has all that – oh!'

'Get it?' urged Cleo.

'And I wouldn't really have to take the job? I mean after a couple of days I could say it wasn't for me?'

'Sure, no problem,' Cleo replied airily. 'Only on Wednesday morning you have to do mine as well – on your own.'

Five minutes later . . . Between mouthfuls

Tansy swallowed hard and bit into the waffle. 'So what's with this audition?' she asked, once they'd finally got to Cleo's news.

Cleo pulled her chair closer to the table and leaned towards Tansy. 'You've seen *Pop Idol*?'

Tansy nodded. 'Hasn't everyone?'

'Well,' Cleo gabbled, 'there's going to be a new show for groups and bands on TV-K – called *WaveBand*. And on Wednesday they will be auditioning for the East Midlands right here in Dunchester.'

'Wow!' This was better. Tansy was actually beginning to look impressed.

'And Angus asked me to sing with them!' Cleo finished, a huge grin spreading across her face. 'In fact, he positively pleaded with me. And if we get through the first round, the final will be on Saturday at Rock Hard, and whoever gets the most votes at Rock Hard goes forward to the show!'

Tansy sighed. 'Remember in Year Nine when I was in the school team for that *Go For It!* programme. That's when I first started fancying Andy . . .' Her voice trailed off and she pushed her plate away.

'So you see you have to do my paper round,' pleaded Cleo, desperate to prevent Tansy from sinking into another bout of misery. 'We have to be at the theatre by eight-thirty in the morning – we're in the first batch to be auditioned.'

'Well . . .'

'And just think,' Cleo raced on. 'Andy won't be able to avoid you will he? Not at eight in the morning. And by Saturday you two will be back on track.'

'All right.' Tansy nodded. 'I'll do it. But only till this audition thing is over, right?'

'Of course,' said Cleo, grinning. 'You can come with me this evening and get me into Mrs P's good books! Oh, and not a word to your mum, right?'

'Why?'

'Because,' Cleo reminded her, 'she works with Kyle's mum. And Kyle's in the band. If my mum gets to hear about it – and you know how she gossips with yours on the phone - you can bet that Killjoys Incorporated will sabotage my career before it's even got off the ground.'

9.30 a.m.
53 Lime Avenue, Oak Hill. The way out!

'Jade! Telephone!'

Jade had just stuffed her mouth full of Oat Krunchies and sliced banana, when Allegra burst into the kitchen, waving the cordless phone.

'Who-ish-it?' Jade mumbled, milk dribbling down her chin.

'Your gran,' Allegra said, chucking the handset on to the kitchen table and snitching a slice of banana from Jade's bowl. 'She sounds a bit odd.'

Jade's heart lurched as she grabbed the telephone. 'Hello? Gran? Are you OK?'

She stuck a finger in her ear to blot out the sounds of Helen's tenth attempt at 'When the Saints Go Marching In' on her trumpet.

'I'm not OK . . .'

A lump appeared in Jade's throat.

'I'm hunky-dory, over the moon, on cloud nine . . .' Her grandmother burst into peals of laughter and every muscle in Jade's body relaxed. Ever since her mum and dad had died, she dreaded losing her gran as well. Certainly today she didn't sound like someone who was on their last legs.

'What's happened?' she said, laughing.

'I won!' her gran cried. 'Jade darling, I WON!'

Jade frowned. 'Won what, Gran?'

'Oh, of course, you don't know anything about it, do you? Silly me – well, there was this prize draw, you see, in aid of Barnardos, and so I bought three tickets and one of them has won me a trip to Paris!'

'Wow!' Jade breathed. 'How cool is that?'

'I'm glad you think so, angel face, because you're coming with me!' Her gran laughed.

'Me? With you?'

'Well, don't make it sound such an ordeal, darling,' her gran teased. 'I may be seventy-three but I'm game for a good time, you know.'

'I didn't mean it like that, Gran,' Jade said. 'It's just – well, school . . .'

'Oh no!' Her gran sounded dejected. 'And I had it in my head that this week was your half-term.'

'It is,' Jade said. 'You mean, we're going so soon?'

'We go on Wednesday and we're back really late on Friday. Only two days, I know, and totally off-season, but what can you expect for a fifty pence raffle ticket!'

'And I can really come?'

'I wouldn't dream of taking anyone else,' her gran said. 'For one thing, I adore you, for another you know how to say "Two coffees and some very large cakes" in French!' Jade giggled. 'And anyway, I thought it would be good for us to be together on Thursday,' her gran added softly.

She took a deep breath and lightened her tone. 'So you'd better come down to Brighton tomorrow. We've got a very early ticket on the Eurostar on Wednesday, and I've booked a taxi for five a.m. to get us to Ashford.'

'That is so exciting,' Jade exclaimed and then drew breath as an amazing thought struck her. 'And, Gran, can I stay at your place on Saturday as well?'

'You can stay as long as you like, darling,' her gran assured her.

That, thought Jade, was precisely what I hoped you would say. She could already hear herself talking to her mates. 'I know it's such a bummer missing Rock Hard, but I'll be in Paris with my grandmother.' Excuses didn't get much more stylish than that.

9.35 a.m.
6 Kestrel Close. Being interrupted

'Cleo, what are you doing on the phone?' Roy thundered down the stairs, tie awry and his jacket over one arm.

'Ringing work,' Cleo replied. 'Or at least I would have been if you hadn't interrupted.'

'I've told you a dozen times before,' her stepfather retorted. 'You have your own mobile – use that.'

'I've run out of credit,' Cleo replied.

'So go to the shop and get a top-up card.'

'It's raining.' Cleo sighed. 'Hard.'

'Oh, hell!' Roy burst out, striding across to the window and peering out in disgust. 'That's all I flaming need!'

'Language, language,' teased Cleo. 'Where's mum?'

'Taking Lettie to her riding lesson,' he told her. 'Though who would want to ride in this weather . . .'

'They have an indoor arena,' Cleo reminded him.

'No wonder they're so expensive,' Roy said, sighing. 'Seventeen pounds an hour and for what? If you ask me . . .'

'Shouldn't you have gone to work by now?' Cleo cut in. 'It's half past nine.'

'What? Oh I've got a meeting,' he told her. 'Over in Milton Keynes. No point going all the way to the office in Bedford to come back again, is there?'

He grabbed his umbrella from the hall stand and turned to face Cleo. 'And don't you go using that phone the moment my back is turned,' he ordered, opening the front door. 'When I was a kid . . .'

10.15 a.m.
Holly's house. Full frontal confrontation

'Sorry I'm late,' Cleo panted, as Holly opened the front door. 'I had to wait for Mum to get back.'

'How could you not tell me?' Holly cut in. 'I thought we were supposed to be mates.'

'Tell you what?' Cleo panted, edging past a large cardboard packing case.

'About Angus . . .'

'How do you know about that?' Cleo stammered. 'Who told you?'

'Angus, actually,' Holly told her. 'Well, no – it was his mum, really.'

'His *mum*?'

'Yes, and considering you knew how much I wanted to get it together with Kyle, you could at least have told me.'

'Hang on a minute,' Cleo butted in. 'You know Kyle's gay and . . .'

'No!' Holly shouted. 'That's precisely what I don't know. We thought he was, we thought he and Angus were an item, but obviously we got it wrong.' She glared at Cleo. 'As clearly you know only too well.'

'Holly, you're not making any sense,' Cleo protested.

Holly shoved Cleo on to the bed and sat down beside her. 'Listen, at the party, Kyle said that wherever he goes, Angus goes, right?'

Cleo nodded.

'And Jade told everyone that meant they were a couple, but if they were then you wouldn't be doing what you're

2 7

doing and Angus's mum wouldn't have said what she said this morning.'

'This morning? What are you on about?'

'OK, I'll start from the beginning. You know we're moving house? Well the Walkers are buying our place and this morning they came round . . .'

Five minutes later . . .

'Oh, boy! Oh wow! Oh my God!'

Cleo stared open-mouthed at Holly. 'So do you think that if I come on to him really strong on Wednesday, I'm in with a chance? And then if we got through to Saturday, I could . . .'

'Hang on,' Holly cut in. 'What's happening on Wednesday.'

Cleo grinned. 'Just wait till you hear this,' she began. 'It will totally blow your mind.'

11.00 a.m.
Priorities, please

'Paula, I'm going to Paris. Gran phoned, and we're leaving on Wednesday!' Jade had rushed to the front door the moment her aunt returned from the supermarket.

'I know,' Paula said, laughing. 'Your gran told me a couple of weeks ago but I was sworn to secrecy. I'm thrilled for you.' She dumped a couple of carrier bags on the floor. 'Now then, you'll need to check that you've got your passport, and you can get some Euros from the bank – and then you need to take a first aid kit, but I don't have to tell you that, and do you think a hot-water bottle would be a good idea? Hotel beds can be a bit damp, you know.'

'Paula?'

'Yes, dear?'

'Can I borrow some money for a new pair of jeans?'

11.35 a.m.
Art appreciation

'Wow, Holly, this is stunning!' Cleo waved a sketchbook in her friend's face. 'Is this your art coursework?'

'Oh, that – it's just the developmental sketches for my 3D-model,' she replied. 'I'm doing this papier-mâché thing. I'm calling it "Agony in Action".'

Modelled on my life, she thought with a sigh. She pulled open a cupboard door and lifted out a half-finished model.

'Oh my God,' Cleo gasped. 'That is amazing.' She stared at the sculpted face, hands clamped to the eyes, and tears strung on small cotton threads falling from its eyes.

'There's going to be a wheel at the bottom,' Holly explained, 'like the wheel of life – only it's in the airing cupboard drying out.'

'And look at this,' Cleo gasped, flicking the page. '"Self Portrait in Winter" – Holly, you are so clever. I can't draw to save my life.'

'But you're good at all the stuff that matters – maths, science . . .'

'They're easy – just logic – but to be able to draw like this . . .'

'They may be easy for you, clever clogs, but they're not

to me, OK? Now can we shut up about school work and get on?' She snatched the sketchbook from Cleo's hand and surveyed the mess of CDs, books and clothes on the floor.

'Hey, what's up?' Cleo asked. 'I didn't mean to offend you. I just thought . . .'

'It's not you, it's me,' Holly said. 'You know how I used to be OK at stuff? Not a brain box, but adequate? Well, now I'm not.'

'Yes, you are . . .'

'Cleo, don't pretend. You know my grades have dropped; I've gone down a set in maths, and even though I'm doing general science, I'm way behind most people. I am going to fail GCSEs big time.'

'That's ridiculous,' Cleo protested. 'You're just having a bad patch.'

Holly pulled a face. 'Come on, I don't want to talk about it. Why don't we just bung all this in the "keep" box and go into town?'

'But I thought your mum said we had to clear the lot,' Cleo began, relieved that Holly's outburst was over as soon as it started.

'My mother says lots of things,' Holly assured her. 'That doesn't mean I have to take any notice of them.'

11.50 a.m.
When all else fails, go shopping!

Tansy stared at her mobile phone, willing it to ring. She couldn't send any more texts to Andy – three in one morning was overdrive as it was. Perhaps she could zap a wacky cartoon over to him; she'd got a new photo phone

3 0

just like his at Christmas so they could swap pictures.

'Please God, let him ring!' she prayed. The phone obligingly shrilled. 'Hello?' she gasped. 'Oh, Jade. It's you.'

'No need to sound so thrilled,' Jade said with a laugh. 'Listen, my gran's taking me to Paris!'

'Wow! Lucky you.'

'Tell me about it! Anyway, I need you to come shopping with me. I so need some cool gear and I'm useless at shopping on my own.'

Tansy sighed. 'Actually, I don't feel like it.' She didn't feel like doing anything except talking to Andy. But then again, sitting at home feeling miserable, or trying to revise her chemistry was no fun either. 'Oh, all right then.'

'Meet me at twelve-thirty outside the bus station, OK?' Jade cut in. '*A bientôt, ma petite!*'

12 noon
This could be the start of something big. Please

'Hang on, my phone's ringing.' Cleo said, as Holly kicked a box into the corner of the room and opened the bedroom door. Cleo flipped the cover of her phone.

'Hi, gorgeous – what are you up to?' Angus shouted down the phone, so loudly that Holly could hear every word.

'I – er – just chilling out,' Cleo stammered, giving Holly the thumbs up sign as the word 'gorgeous' reverberated in her head.

'Cool,' he replied. 'Listen, great news. The *Evening Telegraph* wants to do a piece on the band! Photographs and everything.'

'That's brilliant,' Cleo enthused, as Holly took a step back and leaned in to eavesdrop.

'They're coming to college at lunchtime tomorrow, right? So can you be there?'

'Me?'

'Well, of course you,' Angus said with a laugh. 'You're our lead singer – like we have any others!'

'Of course I'll be there,' she assured him.

'You're a star!' He raised his voice to such a pitch that Cleo had to hold the phone away from her ear. 'And make sure you wear your sexiest outfit, OK? Show them all your best bits!'

'Sure.' Cleo felt her face flush.

'See you at twelve o'clock tomorrow then! Don't be late.'

Two minutes later . . . Parental interruptions

'Just a minute, you two, where do you think you're going?' Holly's mother crawled out from the under-stairs cupboard, her hair even greyer than usual with dust.

'Shopping,' Holly replied, zipping up her jacket. 'Like I said.'

'And what about clearing your room?'

'All done,' Holly replied sweetly. 'More or less.'

Mrs Vine struggled to her feet and rubbed her back. 'And knowing you it will be less rather than more,' she said, smiling. 'So if you don't mind, I'll just check . . . oh, for heaven's sake!' She was interrupted by a loud knock on the front door.

'Mrs Vine? Lance Phillpot, MBM Removals.' A broad

3 2

shouldered guy reached out a gloved hand. 'You asked for an estimate?'

'Oh my goodness!' Holly's mother gasped. 'But I said twelve o'clock . . .'

'It is twelve o'clock, madam,' Mr Phillpot replied with a faint sigh.

'It is? Well, how did that happen?' Mrs Vine glanced at her watch in disbelief.

'Don't worry,' Holly said cheerfully, grinning at Mr Phillpot. 'She lives on another planet. Just be gentle with her, OK? See you later, Mum! Bye!'

1.10 p.m.

Tansy stared out of the window of Olé Outfitters as she waited for Jade to emerge from the changing cubicles. Suddenly, a figure caught her eye. It wasn't – it couldn't be. Could it?

'So what do you think? The bootleg ones or these?' Jade twirled round in a pair of hipsters. 'Tansy?'

'What?' She glanced at her friend. 'Oh, sorry. Either. Both. Nice.'

'What's with you today?' Jade demanded. 'Ever since you got here you've been a million miles away. I might as well have come on my own for all the help you are.'

'I'm sorry – get the hipsters,' Tansy muttered, turning back to the window. 'They're really classy.'

'OK, so now I need a top to go with them,' Jade said, heading towards a rail marked 'New Season – Just In' by the window. 'Just one – Gran said she'd get me something really chic when we get to Paris and . . . Tansy, where are you going?'

'Hang on, I'll be right back.' Tansy dodged a woman with a buggy and ran out of the shop. She glanced to left and right round the crowded mall and then broke into a run. The guy had his back to her but she knew it was him by the way he walked with one hand stuffed in the pocket of his parka and the other hooked round the back of his neck. He always did that when he was stressed out.

'Andy, wait!' He was just about to step into the glass-walled lift. She had to stop him. 'Andy, wait!' She shouted again at the top of her voice. He turned briefly, and even at fifty metres' distance she could see the colour flood his face. He looked a mess; his hair was sticking up on end and his glasses seemed to be held together with sticking plaster. But right then, she could have hugged him just for being there.

'Hi!' She waved and dodged round a couple of old ladies blocking her path.

At that moment, the lift doors opened and Andy stepped inside.

'Hang on! Excuse me!' She belted to the lift doors and only just resisted the temptation to elbow a couple of women out of the way.

'Sorry, love, it's full.' One of the women gestured towards the notice that read 'Ten People Maximum'.

'I'll catch you on the next floor, right?' There was no time for Andy to reply before the doors zapped closed.

Tansy flew along the mall to the escalator, belted up the steps two at a time and careered along to the lift. It had gone and there was no sign of Andy.

'Sugar!' He could be anywhere; he might even have gone on up to the car park where she wouldn't have a hope in hell of finding him. Besides, Jade would be doing her nut.

But at least she knew he was OK. It was as she made her way back to Olé Outfitters that it hit her. Not only had he not replied when she asked him to call her; if he'd wanted to see her he could have waited for the next lift. As it was, he hadn't even smiled.

1.12 p.m.
Clothes encounters

'Do you think I could wear this?' Cleo reached out for a sequined cardigan

'Do you mind?' said a voice. 'I was just going to . . . oh, it's you!'

A hand yanked the cardie away and a freckled face peered over the top of the rail.

'Jade!' Cleo cried, eyeing the carrier bags in her friend's hand. 'Hi. Are you on a spend too?'

'You bet,' Jade replied. 'I'm going to Paris tomorrow and I so need that top!'

'Paris!' Cleo and Holly chorused in unison. 'How come?'

'I'll tell you later, but listen – is this my colour or not?'

'Sure,' said Holly.

'No way,' protested Cleo.

'Great help you are!' Jade sighed. 'Tansy was supposed to be sorting me out, but she's suddenly done a runner and left me. She's been acting odd all morning.'

'She's in a state,' Cleo confided, reaching out for a lacy camisole. 'It's . . .well, I'm not supposed to say anything.'

'But you will,' Holly assured her. 'Won't you?'

Two minutes later . . .

'So that's why she's upset, I guess,' Cleo concluded after telling them the saga of Tansy and Andy.

'I don't believe it,' Jade gasped, running her hand along the rail in search of more clothes, 'I mean, those two have been joined at the hip since for ever.'

'I know.' Cleo nodded, holding the camisole up to her chest and eyeing herself in the mirror. 'Tansy reckons he might have found someone else . . .'

'Come off it,' Holly cut in. 'I mean, Andy's a nice enough guy and all that, but he's hardly eye candy, is he?'

'Well, Tansy's dead cut up about it all anyway,' Cleo said, taking a black-leather miniskirt from the rail. 'She said to me . . .'

'Oh well, that's great, Cleo Greenway! Thanks a lot!'

Cleo whirled round to find Tansy, red faced and out of breath, glaring at her.

'Tansy, I . . .' Cleo stammered, dropping the skirt in her confusion.

'So you've all had a good laugh, have you?' Tansy said. 'You've been . . .'

'Of course we haven't,' Jade cut in, grabbing the skirt from the floor. 'We were just saying that Andy adores you and there must be some other reason that he's acting weird.'

'Really?' Tansy looked slightly mollified.

'Of course,' Holly replied. 'All we need to do is find a way of sussing what's going on.'

'Cleo already did that,' Tansy confessed and proceeded to tell them about the paper round.

'Not,' she said, sighing, 'that it's going to work. From what I've just seen, the last person on earth Andy Richards is interested in is me.'

1.20 p.m

'Come on, Tansy, cheer up – there could be a zillion reasons why he's acting funny,' Holly insisted. 'Why don't you stop thinking about it and come for lunch with us?'

'I'm not hungry,' said Tansy. 'I think I'll go home. After all, he might call me to explain . . .'

'So – you've got your mobile,' Jade said.

'Besides, he might still be hanging out somewhere in the mall,' Holly added. 'You might bump into him again.'

'Oh, all right then,' Tansy said. 'Look, I'm just going outside to get a better signal on my phone, just in case there's a text.'

Cleo stared after her as she marched out of the shop. 'I don't get it,' she murmured. 'Tansy's always so laid back about life. She's never been like this over a guy before – I guess she really must love him.'

'You know what I think?' Jade mused. 'I reckon that after all that business with her real dad not wanting to know her, this feels like yet another rejection.'

'You could be right.' Cleo nodded.

'So you think Andy really is giving her the brush-off?' Holly asked.

Jade shrugged. 'How do I know? I just think we should be there for her right now.'

1.27 p.m.

'OK, so it's my slinky dress for Saturday, and these cool hipsters for Wednesday, which means I just have to have this cardigan for the photo shoot!' Cleo whipped the sequined top from Jade's hand.

'Hang on,' Jade protested. 'That's the only one in my size.' She paused. 'Did you say photo shoot?'

'I did,' Cleo cried triumphantly. 'With the band. And I rather think my big career break wins over a trip to France, don't you?'

'What is she on about?' Jade asked, turning to Holly as Cleo shot off to the cash desk. 'She's not usually that up herself.'

'She is these days . . .' Holly proceeded to give Jade the low-down on the band's audition.

'Still,' she concluded, 'I guess it'll be cool if they get through to the final on Saturday at Rock Hard. Are you bringing anyone?'

'I can't come,' Jade said. 'I'll be in Paris.'

'Oh no,' gasped Holly. 'And it's going to be such a brilliant evening.'

'I know. I'm gutted. Really I am.'

2.45 p.m.

'See you at the newsagent's at five!' Cleo called to Tansy as she jumped off the bus at her stop. 'And don't look so miserable – we'll get this all sorted.'

Tansy gave her a half-hearted wave and turned to Holly. 'Do you think maybe I should call him just once more?' she asked.

'No, I don't,' Holly replied firmly as the bus pulled away, 'I think I should.'

'You?'

'Yes, because if he is avoiding you, and sees your number come up, he'll ignore it,' Holly began.

'Do you think that's what he's doing?' Tansy looked mortified.

'I didn't say that,' Holly stressed, 'but if he is, then seeing my number come up on the screen won't mean a thing, will it? What's his number?'

'07950 7277345,' Tansy dictated. 'But don't you dare let him think I care!'

Holly punched in the number.

'The Vodafone you are calling is switched off . . .'

'Sugar,' Holly muttered. 'Never mind, let's try his home phone.'

Tansy leaned close to Holly in order to hear what went on. Within seconds, the phone was answered.

'Melanie - is that you?' The voice was unmistakably Andy's.

'Melanie?' Tansy's face paled as she whispered the name. 'Who the hell is Melanie?'

'No, it's me, Holly Vine,' said Holly firmly. 'Is Tansy with you?'

'Oh. Tansy? No, she's not,' Andy said. 'Look, I can't talk . . .'

'So when will you be seeing her?' Holly demanded.

'I don't know - next week at school, I guess. Sorry, I've got to go, OK?'

The phone went dead.

'I did try,' Holly whispered as Tansy turned to stare

out of the bus window. 'Perhaps he's just got family problems – you know, like before?'

'Really?' Holly could hear the sarcasm in Tansy's voice. 'A family problem called Melanie? I don't think so.'

3.00 p.m.

'Mum, I'm home!' Cleo called as the front door slammed behind her. 'Where are you?'

'She's on the phone.' Lettie, Cleo's twelve-year-old sister stuck her head round the sitting-room door. 'Having a row with her agent. Listen.'

Cleo threw her jacket on to the stairs and edged nearer the study door.

'Now you just listen to me,' she heard her mother shout, 'You are my agent and you've done pretty damn well out of me over the years. It's your job to find me a part . . . what do you mean, not many roles for someone like me?'

Cleo could hear her mother's breathing becoming more laboured.

'I have never heard such a ridiculous comment in my life!' she stormed. 'The reason I haven't had any big parts in recent years is because you aren't doing your job properly.'

'Put the kettle on,' Cleo mouthed to Lettie. 'Crisis brewing.'

4.00 p.m.
Noises off

'What,' Holly asked in alarm, as she helped her mother tape up yet another box on the landing, 'is that awful noise?'

'Your father,' her mother replied. 'He's in the attic

sorting through his old Civil War stuff and – oh my goodness!'

There was an enormous thud, followed by a series of words that Holly would have been grounded for uttering.

'Rupert? Rupert, are you all right?' Holly's mum rushed along the landing and yelled up into the loft.

'No, I am not bloody all right!' her father stormed above the sound of yet another crash. 'Tripped over some piece of dratted wire. Clobbered my knee. Ridiculous place to have wires!'

'Shall I make you some tea?' his wife volunteered as he appeared at the top of the loft ladder, red in the face and rubbing his leg.

'Tea? Double scotch and soda, more like,' he grunted, rubbing his knee and wincing. 'I'm done for the day. Had enough.'

'All right, dear,' Holly's mum agreed soothingly. 'Just hand me down the rubbish and we'll call it quits.'

Rupert turned back and passed a black bin bag to his wife.

'And the next one,' she called cheerfully.

'There isn't a next one,' he said. 'That's the lot. Everything else I keep.'

'For goodness' sake, Rupert,' his wife exploded. 'We are downsizing – there won't be any space.'

'I've worked that out,' Rupert said smugly. 'All my pikestaffs and helmets can go on the walls instead of pictures, and I thought the armour could stand in the hall as a feature.'

Holly looked at her mother. Her mother looked back.

'Pour your father a Scotch, darling,' Angela said firmly. 'I think his tumble has affected his brain.'

4.30 p.m.

'Oh, bother!' Cleo's mum slammed the phone down on the table. 'Where is that man?'

'Who?' asked Cleo, spreading peanut butter on to a rice cake.

'Roy,' her mother replied. 'I want him to pick up some dry cleaning on his way home but his mobile is switched off.'

'So call his secretary,' suggested Cleo. 'She's the one who organises him!'

'Do it for me, darling,' pleaded her mum. 'I'm going upstairs to freshen up.'

Like I haven't anything else to do, thought Cleo, punching her stepfather's office number into the phone. 'Hi, is that Donna? It's Cleo Greenway – can I leave a message for my stepdad?'

'Roy?' the secretary replied. 'Well, he's not here, dear. Surely he told you . . .?'

'Oh, I forgot. Milton Keynes,' Cleo replied. 'Sorry to have bothered you.' She ran upstairs and told her mum.

'Milton Keynes?' Mrs Greenway paused, her hand on her forehead. 'He never told me. What a shame – I could have gone with him for a little shopping spree.'

'That,' Cleo said with a smile, 'is probably why he didn't say a word.'

5.45 p.m.

'Now, this is what we do,' Cleo instructed Tansy as they reached Andy's house. 'You put this paper through the door, right?'

'But this one says number 43, and Andy is number 41,' Tansy protested.

'Do I have to spell it out?' said Cleo. 'Put the wrong one through and you get to ring the doorbell, apologise profusely and ask for it back.'

'I get it,' Tansy gasped. 'And then what?'

'Then,' stressed Cleo, 'it's up to you. I'll go off and do the rest of the street while you deal with your love life. You've got ten minutes.' With that she hurried across the road, satchel over her shoulder.

Please be there, Tansy prayed silently, her finger on the doorbell. From inside the house she could hear a baby crying but no one came to the door. She tried again, rattling the letterbox for good measure. A curtain twitched in an upstairs room, and then she heard the sound of footsteps on the stairs.

'Yes?' The door was opened half a centimetre and an elderly woman with greying hair and rather prominent bristles on her pointed chin peered out.

'Oh.' Tansy was taken aback by the stranger. 'I'm so sorry to bother you – I'm afraid I pushed the wrong newspaper through your door by mistake.'

'No problem,' the woman said, stooping to pick it up. 'There you are.'

'Thanks.' Tansy hesitated as the baby's cries grew more urgent. 'Um – is Andy in?'

'No,' the woman said, taking the right newspaper from Tansy's outstretched hand. 'Been out all day.'

'His mum?' Tansy was getting desperate.

'They're all out,' the woman said. 'Well, except the twins. I'm babysitting. Sorry, got to go; it's feeding time.'

'Can you get Andy to call Tansy when he gets back?' Tansy didn't mean to sound so desperate but she couldn't help it. 'Could you say . . .?'

But the woman had already shut the door.

7.00 p.m.
In the dark – in more ways than one

'Whose turn is it to load the dishwasher?' Paula asked at the end of supper.

'Mine.' Allegra sighed.

'I'll do it for you,' Jade blurted out hurriedly. 'And Helen, I'll do your chores too, OK?'

'Like, why?' Allegra said. 'What's the catch?'

'No catch,' Jade smiled. 'I just want a word with Paula.'

'Darling, what's wrong?' Paula asked anxiously as Allegra and Helen scooted out of the kitchen as fast as they could.

'I just wanted to talk about Mum and Dad,' Jade said softly. 'I mean, I'll be in France on Thursday and I know you'll be thinking about Mum and . . .'

'I think about her every day,' Paula admitted. 'I'm glad you're going away – it'll take your mind off it.'

Jade held her gaze and her aunt dropped her eyes.

'That was a dumb thing to say,' she said, sighing. 'Of course it won't, but at least your gran – oh no! What's happened?'

The whole kitchen plunged into darkness. 'Mum, the TV's gone off,' Helen shouted. 'I can't see a thing.'

Jade sighed. Just as she was about to get to the serious bit of the conversation. Typical.

'Jade darling, can you look and see if there are any lights on over the road?' Paula asked, scrabbling in a drawer. 'I'm sure I had some candles somewhere.'

'Everything's pitch black,' Jade said. 'The whole road's out. Don't worry, there's a torch in my room. I'll get it.'

It doesn't matter, she thought as she felt her way up the stairs and into her bedroom. It was probably a stupid question anyway. Best to forget all about it.

7.30 p.m.

'Holly, shouldn't you be doing your homework instead of sitting there texting on that wretched phone?' her father asked, limping into the room and gesturing to the pile of coursework on the coffee table.

'Dad, in case you hadn't noticed, there is a power cut. That means no lights. That means I can't see to do – oh!'

The lights zapped back on, the TV blared with renewed vigour and the bars of the electric fire began to glow orange.

'And now you can!' her father exclaimed triumphantly, as Holly jumped up and headed for the door. 'So where do you think you are off to now?'

'The loo, OK?' Holly retorted. 'I assume I am allowed to answer the call of nature?'

'Of course,' her father replied sweetly. 'But blow out the candles as you go – oh, and you won't be needing your phone in the loo, will you?'

11.50 p.m.
Sweet dreams of stardom

The spotlight fell on Cleo. She stepped to the edge of the stage. She hit a top C and the audience broke into rapturous applause. Angus turned and kissed her full on the lips.

Cleo threw her arms in the air. And fell out of bed.

11.51 p.m.
Less sweet dreams of exams

'Turn over your papers; you may begin.'

Holly eyed the enormous clock on the wall and turned over her maths paper. It was covered in extraordinary writing that seemed to be a mixture of hieroglyphics and bus timetables.

'Please, sir. I don't understand,' she gasped, putting up her hand to attract the attention of Mr. Boardman.

'You don't understand anything, Holly Vine,' he shouted. 'You are sure to fail.'

'Fail, fail, fail,' chanted the rest of the students, pointing their pens at her. 'She can't do it, she can't do it . . .'

'*No!*' Holly woke up with a shriek, her face wet with tears.

11.54 p.m.
Tossing and turning

Tomorrow. I'll see him tomorrow, Tansy told herself, pummelling her pillow in an attempt to get comfortable. And I'm going to be really cool and laid back. Then again, not too laid back in case he thinks I'm doing fine without him. But then again, I'm not going to let him see that I'm in pieces and I love him so much and . . .

Who the hell is that Melanie?

11.59 p.m.
More dreams?

'Paris!' breathed Jade's gran, taking her arm and pointing to the Eiffel Tower, lit up against the night sky. 'Let's go up there right now.' She took Jade's hand and for some inexplicable reason, they found themselves flying high above the River Seine.

'Jade, darling, you came!' Jade's mum, dressed in her favourite blue dress with the tiny pearl buttons, opened her arms and Jade fell into them.

'Mum! You're here.'

'Of course I'm here,' her mother said, laughing. 'I'm always here – wherever you go. Don't forget that, will you?'

Jade squeezed her mum tight. But there was nothing in her arms. Her mum had disappeared.

She woke up, clutching her pillow to her chest and sobbed.

TUESDAY

7.20 a.m
On the freezing streets of Dunchester

'I looked back, couldn't relax, red eyes full of anger / Life a mess, only stress . . .'

It wasn't till she saw a couple of businessmen in dark suits eyeing her curiously that Cleo realised she was actually skipping down the road, singing at the top of her voice. Normally, she would have cringed with embarrassment, but right now she didn't care; she'd been working on this new song for days and suddenly it was bursting out of her brain.

'Now I've changed, my directions rearranged, the past is gone and the present makes my fu-oooo-ture . . .'

'Cleo! Wait!'

Tansy came panting up behind her. 'I've been yelling at you for the last three minutes.' She laughed. 'What are you on?'

'Sorry,' Cleo said. 'It's my song – I was trying it out.'

'The one you're going to sing tomorrow?'

Cleo shook her head. 'No, the one I'm writing – mind you, it's only two verses so far.'

'You are so clever,' Tansy gasped. 'Did you write the tune and everything?'

Cleo nodded. 'It just came into my head the other day,' she admitted. 'Trouble is, there are bits I just can't get right.'

'So get Angus to help, why don't you? He's a music student, isn't he?' suggested Tansy. She winked at Cleo.

'You could put your heads together in an intimate fashion . . . '

Cleo gawped at her. 'Tansy Meadows,' she gasped. 'You are a genius.'

'Geniuses,' Tansy said with a sigh, 'do not get out of bed at seven in the morning to pace the freezing streets with a load of newspapers. Come on, let's get it over and done with before it starts to snow.'

8.05 a.m
Outside Andy's house

'OK, I'll grab the papers for these three houses,' Cleo told Tansy as they turned the corner into Ridings Way. 'You do from the bus shelter down to Andy's house and – oh my God!' She stopped dead, her eyes widening. 'Look!' She pointed past the bus shelter to Andy's house. Parked outside was a police patrol car.

'Oh no, what's happened?' Tansy's voice was shrill with panic. 'Go on, find out!'

'I can't just go barging in,' Cleo protested. 'You're the one who knows the family – you go.'

'Do you think they've been burgled?' Tansy said. 'Or attacked in their beds?'

'It's probably nothing,' Cleo assured her.

'Oh sure, like the police go round calling on people before breakfast just for the sheer hell of it,' Tansy retorted.

'Well,' Cleo reasoned, thrusting the bag of papers at her, 'there's only one way to find out.'

Two minutes later . . .

Tansy walked up the path as slowly as she dared, craning her neck to peer into the front room. There was a light on, but the room was empty.

Before she realised she was doing it, she dropped the *Financial Times* on to the sodden pathway and gave it a kick for good measure. Eyeing the dirty patch on the back page with satisfaction, she pressed the bell.

'No, I'll get it!' An unfamiliar voice echoed down the hallway and she heard the latch being lifted.

A tall policewoman with ash-blond hair opened the door. 'Yes?'

Sugar, thought Tansy. She took a deep breath. 'Um – could I speak to Mr or Mrs Richards?' She reckoned that sounded more plausible than asking for Andy right now.

'I'm sorry, not at the moment. Shall I take those?' She reached for the papers in Tansy's hand.

'I dropped them – I really need to speak to the house-holders,' she insisted in the most business like voice she could manage.

'Tansy! What are you doing here?' Her heart lifted as she peered over the policewoman's left shoulder and saw Andy coming down the stairs.

'Andy! What's going on? Are you OK? I've been so worried.' She tried to push past the policewoman but her way was blocked.

'I can't talk to you now, right?' Andy's voice sounded brittle.

'But what's happening? You didn't answer my texts.'

'Tansy, I said not now, OK?' Andy cut in. 'I'll – I'll call you later.'

The policewoman took the newspapers and began closing the front door.

'Promise?' Tansy called. 'Promise me you'll call? Soon?'

Andy was already turning away. 'Yeah, yeah, whatever,' he muttered.

It was not quite the enthusiastic reply that Tansy had hoped for but it was better than nothing. At least she'd find out the truth once and for all.

Ten minutes later . . .

'Look at it this way,' said Cleo, as they shoved the final newspaper through the door of a dilapidated cottage, 'No one's been murdered because they didn't put that blue-and-white tape stuff round the house, Andy's in one piece and he's going to call you.'

'I guess,' Tansy replied, pulling her scarf across her mouth as snow began to fall in large flakes.

'So if you don't mind, I've got to get off home and glam up for the photo shoot. What are you doing today?'

'Homework,' said Tansy. 'Not that I can concentrate on anything right now.'

'So come to the photo shoot with me, then,' Cleo offered. 'To be honest, I'm really nervous about going on my own.'

That was a lie, but she knew just how rough Tansy was feeling and having been to hell and back herself when she split with Trig the year before, she was sure moping was the worst thing to do.

'I don't know,' said Tansy, sighing.

'No excuses,' Cleo urged. 'Bring your phone and check

for texts every ten seconds if you like. Just come. Please?'

'OK,' Tansy said with a nod. 'See you there.'

9.05 a.m.
Paternal apoplexy

'I simply don't believe this! It's outrageous!' Holly's father thumped the table so hard that the milk in her bowl of Oat Krunchies splashed on to the cloth.

'What's the matter, dear?' her mother asked calmly.

'This quote from the removal men,' he stormed. 'Nine hundred and forty-five pounds for moving us five miles! I've never heard anything so ridiculous in my life.'

'Never mind,' his wife replied sweetly. 'There's a simple solution. The less we take with us, dear, the less it will cost. Now, about those pikestaffs and the suit of armour . . .'

'Actually, nine hundred and forty-five pounds is not a bad deal when you think about it,' her husband stressed. 'I'll call them and accept when I get to the museum.' He kissed the top of Holly's head. 'I trust you are going to do some revision today, Holly,' he went on. 'This is a very . . .'

'Important year,' Holly said with a sigh. 'I know. You mentioned it.'

'So what are your plans?' her mother asked as her father shut the door behind him. 'I shall be out all morning but that doesn't mean you can loll around.'

'Mum, leave it out, OK?' Holly replied. 'I'm going to finish my model for art, OK?'

'Well, I suppose the sooner you finish that, the sooner you'll start on the stuff that really matters.'

'That is such a narrow viewpoint,' Holly stormed. 'Just because you think art is a cop-out . . .'

'No, I don't,' her mother butted in. 'It's just that maths and science and stuff like that are essential if you're going to make anything of your life.'

'Well, I'm probably not!' To her horror, Holly felt her eyes fill with tears. 'I'm probably going to be a total failure, so you might as well get used to it, OK?'

She ran out of the room, slamming the door behind her. Thundering up the stairs two at a time, she burst into her bedroom and punched the On button on her sound system. The latest Luminous Igloo hit blared out so loudly that she didn't realise her mum had come into the room till she felt a pair of strong arms wrap themselves round her from behind.

'Holly Vine,' her mum said, giving her a squeeze, 'you are not and never will be a failure. Get it?'

That did it. Holly turned round and laid her head on her mum's shoulder and sobbed. 'Mum, I can't do it. Something's happened to my brain. I can't do it any more.'

10.00 a.m.
At Dunchester Station, being fussed over

'Now darling, you've got your passport? And your Euros?' Paula peered anxiously into Jade's bag for the tenth time. 'Make sure you sit next to someone respectable looking on the train.'

'I'll be fine, Paula, honestly. I'm going to Brighton – it's hardly a walk on the wild side!'

Paula sighed. 'You can't be too careful,' she stressed.

'Oh, and your gran said you should get a taxi from Brighton Station to her flat. Have you got enough cash?'

'Plenty,' Jade assured her as the train pulled into the station. 'Stop worrying. I'll call you when I get to gran's, OK?'

'You do that – and have a lovely time, darling!' Her aunt gave her a hug.

Jade climbed on to the train.

'Look, I've got to dash,' Paula said. 'Just have a great time – oh, and don't talk to strangers!'

'Sssh!' Jade put her finger to her lips, cringing with embarrassment at her aunt's strident tones. To her relief, Paula gave a final wave and ran back towards the car park.

She was on her own. And for the next three days she wouldn't have to put on an act and pretend to be something she wasn't. It felt very good.

11.40 a.m.
Trackside traumas

'Hang on – don't go! Please, can someone help?'

Jade looked up from her book to see a dark-skinned boy with curly hair and worried brown eyes manipulating his wheelchair towards the train door and looking frantically up and down the platform. She stuffed her book into her bag, jumped up and went to the door.

'Are you OK? Do you need any help?' she asked.

'They're supposed to come with a ramp,' he said. 'But I can't see anyone, and it looks like the train's about to leave.'

'Don't worry,' Jade cut in. She put one foot on the platform and the other on the step. 'They can't go now, can they?' She looked across to the information office just as a station attendant appeared wheeling the ramp.

'Sorry to have kept you,' he said to the boy. 'Some idiot had stored this in the wrong place. Now then, you happy to be in this coach?'

'Yes, fine.' The boy looked relieved. 'And there will be someone to help me off when we get to London, won't there?'

'I'll make sure of it,' the attendant said. 'I'll phone through the moment the train leaves.'

'I'm going to London too,' Jade added, 'so I can help.'

'Thanks!' The boy smiled as he manoeuvred the chair up the ramp and the doors closed behind them. 'To be honest, this is the first time I've travelled by train on my own in my new chair and I'm still getting used to handling it.'

He paused as he positioned his chair in the bay marked 'Wheelchairs Only'. It was, thought Jade, quite a change to met a guy who didn't put on the usual macho image the moment he saw a girl.

'No way,' she said. 'To be honest, I'm pretty nervous about finding my way to the Thameslink station on my own and I'm not in a wheelchair.'

'You're going there? So am I! That's brilliant – well, it is for me,' the guy exclaimed. 'I'm going to Sussex to see my sister. She's at uni down in Brighton.'

'That's great, because that's where I'm going, so I can help you,' Jade said. 'I mean – if you want me to.' She was aware that she sounded horribly patronising. 'Not that you need it, of course, but . . .'

'That would be cool,' the guy replied easily. 'I'm Flynn, by the way.'

'I'm Jade,' said Jade, grabbing hold of the handrail as the train lurched over some points.

'Oh gosh, I'm sorry, you'll be wanting to get back to your seat. I'm fine now, honestly.'

'I was sitting here anyway,' Jade told him, flopping into the vacant seat next to Flynn's chair.

She spent the next few moments trying to work out why she had bothered to make up a lie to someone she had known only for four minutes.

Meanwhile, diverted to Holly's house, with a whole heap of tissues . . .

'I just can't believe it,' Tansy sobbed, leaning her elbows on the kitchen table. 'How could he just end it like that – no explanation, nothing.'

IT'S TIME YOU KNEW – IT'S OVER BETWEEN US. SO STOP HASSLING ME. A.

Holly read out the message for the third time and shook her head in bewilderment. 'I just don't get it.'

'I do,' hiccuped Tansy, wiping her eyes on a crumpled tissue. 'He's met someone else – it's obvious. This Melanie person, I bet.'

'The only Melanie I can think of is Ella I'm-Up-My-Own-Backside Hankinson's sister,' Holly commented.

'Oh my God.' Tansy's mouth dropped open and her face paled. 'He couldn't have – he wouldn't – he said he didn't want to and I said neither did I, but then – he wouldn't have, would he?'

'Hang on,' Holly interrupted, pushing her art work to

one side as Tansy arms flailed about. 'You've lost me. Could you start at the beginning?'

'Last week, he got this invitation to Ella's party last Saturday . . .'

'Ella invited *him*?' Holly looked gobsmacked.

'Yes, and he said did I mind us not going, because they so don't hit it off. I said I'd rather have root canal work.'

'Naturally,' agreed Holly.

'And then he got ill anyway, and so nothing more was said.'

'Which,' interjected Holly, 'was a happy release. And why would Ella invite Andy to her party? They hardly speak to one another.'

'Use your head,' Tansy retorted. 'Ella's going out with Alex, right? And Alex is one of Andy's best mates.'

'Oh, yes,' recalled Holly. 'So what are you trying to say?'

'What if Andy was bluffing? What if he used the excuse of being ill to stop me going and then . . .'

'He went on his own and got off with Melanie,' Holly concluded, her eyes widening.

'See? You think he did, don't you?' Tansy threw Holly an accusing glance.

'I don't know what to think,' Holly admitted.

'It's too much of a coincidence,' Tansy declared. 'I'm going round there. I'm going to kill her. How dare she, the hateful little cow!'

'Hang on,' Holly interrupted. 'For one thing, we don't know it's her. For another, if it happened – and we don't know that it did – Andy had a part in it, right? It's him you need to sort. Have you replied to the text?'

'Get real,' Tansy snapped. 'I've hardly had time to get my head round it – and then there's this police thing. What's all that about?'

'Probably nothing,' Holly said dismissively. 'Maybe his parents witnessed an accident or something.' She picked up Tansy's phone and shoved it at her. 'Go on, reply to the message,' she urged. 'Say you need to meet up and talk.'

'OK.' Tansy began fingering the keypad just as the phone bleeped.

'No wait – there's another message from him,' she gasped, and Holly couldn't help noticing the hope in her voice.

'Well, what does he say?'

Tansy didn't reply. She merely threw the phone down on the table and burst into floods of tears. And when Holly looked at the screen, she could understand why.

Five minutes later . . .
Full of righteous indignation

'If that's the way he's going to behave, you are well rid of him!' Holly stormed, pacing up and down the kitchen in indignation. 'What a callous thing to do!'

She snatched Tansy's phone for the fifth time and glared at it. Staring back at her was a full face picture of Melanie Hankinson and underneath were the words GET THE MESSAGE?

'Right,' she thundered. 'We need a plan of action. Leave this to me.'

'There's no point,' said Tansy, picking at a bit of loose skin round her thumbnail. 'Anyway, I have to go and meet Cleo.'

'There's every point,' Holly declared. 'You're my friend, you've been hurt and I'm not going to stand by and do nothing. Get it?'

Tansy gave her a watery smile. 'So what are you going to do?'

'I don't know yet,' Holly admitted. 'But I promise you one thing. By the end of today, Andy Richards is going to wish he had never been born.'

11.50 a.m.
In transit

'That was easy,' Jade said as she walked alongside Flynn's electric chair and crossed the concourse of St Pancras Station. 'Now we need to find a lift. Just have to follow the signs to King's Cross Thameslink and . . .'

'Jade, I'm OK,' Flynn stressed. 'My legs may be useless but believe it or not, I have a brain.'

'Sorry,' Jade apologised. 'I didn't mean to sound bossy.'

'It's all right,' Flynn smiled. 'But my mum was right – she said I had to do it all by myself. Good practice, she said.'

'That sounds a bit mean,' Jade said.

Flynn shook his head. 'No, she's right,' he said, heading for the lifts. 'I'll be going to uni in a couple of years and no way do I want to be seen as the poor guy in the wheelchair who needs a minder all the time.'

'Have you always been . . .' Jade hesitated.

'Disabled?' Flynn asked, moving the chair forward. 'No. Two years ago, I was water-skiing when some jerk in a speedboat cut us up. And chopped some nerves in my lower spine.'

'That's awful,' Jade gasped.

'I've had better days,' Flynn said, grinning. 'But it could have been worse. I'm alive, I can walk a little bit with sticks when I have to, I've got some great mates and now?' he looked at her out of the corner of his eye. 'I've got a stunning girl falling over herself to take care of me.'

Jade didn't know whether to snap his head off for arrogance, die of embarrassment, or laugh.

'Actually,' he said as they crossed Pentonville Road and headed to the entrance to the Thameslink Station, 'there *is* something you could do for me.'

'Of course,' she said. 'Get your ticket? Call the lift?'

'Give me your phone number,' he replied. 'Just in case you disappear without trace on the way to Brighton.'

12.05 p.m.
Chat lines

By the time the train had left the city for the red-roofed suburbs, Jade had discovered that Flynn's mum had left Jamaica as a child and come to England with her parents, that his dad was a pilot with EasyJet and that he had two older sisters. He was passionate about sport and chocolate raisins, and loathed cabbage and people who talked to him as if he had half a brain.

By the time they passed Gatwick Airport, she had told him about her parents' deaths, about how she hated the whole party scene and how she wanted to be a nurse in Africa. She even admitted to running away from a field trip in Year Nine and had him in hysterics over the antics of her cousins.

And as the train pulled into Brighton station, she

reflected on how much easier life was when you could talk to someone you knew you would never see again and who you had no need to impress.

'Is someone meeting you?' she asked as the train edged slowly under the wrought-iron roof and on to the platform.

'My sister,' he said with a nod. 'What about you?'

'I'm taking a cab to my grandmother's flat,' she replied, as the train attendant appeared with a mobile ramp and beckoned to Flynn. 'So, it's been good talking to you. Have a great time with your sister.'

'Hang on,' he said, laying an hand on her arm. 'You never gave me that phone number.'

'What? Oh, well . . .'

'Unless, of course, you don't want to.' He averted his eyes and began fiddling with the strap on his bag.

'Sure I do,' she told him, fishing in her bag for a piece of paper and scribbling the number. 'There you go.'

'And here's mine,' he offered, stuffing a Post-it note into the top of her bag.

After Flynn had manoeuvred his chair on to the platform and the attendant had left, he turned to Jade. 'Will the phone work while you're in France?' he asked with a smile.

Jade shrugged. 'I don't know,' she said. 'I never thought about that.'

'Well,' he said, 'we'll soon find out. I'll text you.'

Jade tried to look as if it didn't matter to her whether he did or not. Because it didn't. Did it?

12.10 p.m.
Songs and shocks

'Now I've changed, my directions rearranged. Don't act strange, cos I'm running my life now . . .'

Cleo turned up the collar of her jacket and shimmied down Kestrel Close and into Weston Way. She glanced anxiously at the dark grey clouds. If it starting snowing again, her hair would go all frizzy and ruin her carefully manufactured pop star appearance. She knew she looked good; underneath the jacket her sequined top and cardigan clung in all the right places and the gap between her top and the waistband of her hipsters was suitably seductive. And very chilly. She broke into a run to try to keep warm.

'I won't cry, I've said goodbye and now I've changed direction . . .'

At least she'd managed to get away without having to face a family inquisition about why she was going out all glammed up. Her mother had had another mood crash and gone to bed with a headache, Portia had left for a residential in Wales with college and Lettie was spending the day mucking out at the riding school.

As she crossed the Kettleborough Road and headed up Booth Lane to the college, she slackened her pace. It wouldn't do to turn up looking red-faced and out of breath; she had to cultivate an aura of serenity and calm.

'Deep breaths,' she told herself, echoing the instructions of her singing teacher before every exam. 'Think beautiful thoughts and smile.'

She walked through the college gates and followed the

signs to the Wilson Building. Pushing past a cluster of students, she went through the swing doors and into the foyer. And saw something which banished all attempts at serenity in an instant.

Standing in the far corner, briefcase in hand, was her stepfather in animated conversation with a young woman with auburn hair, wearing a paisley skirt and a lime green poncho.

And as she dodged behind a six-foot rugby-playing type in an attempt to hide, she saw Roy place a hand on the woman's backside and steer her through a door marked 'Private'.

Forty minutes later . . . Pressing matters

'OK, it's a wrap,' the photographer called. 'Just hang on a minute though – our features guy wants to have a few words.' He cupped his hands to his mouth and shouted to a tall, fair-haired guy who was leaning against the college wall and slurping coffee from a polystyrene cup. 'Leo! It's all yours, mate!'

Tansy prodded Holly in the ribs. 'Isn't that the reporter who did that piece about your mum when she dressed up as a rabbit and got arrested?' she asked.

'Would you mind,' hissed Holly, 'keeping your voice down. It's taken me nearly two years to live that down.' She glanced at Leo as he ambled over, notebook in hand. 'Hopefully he won't remember me,' she said, turning away and sidling over to where Kyle, Liam and Angus were packing up their instruments. 'Cool shots, guys – you looked dead professional.'

'Let's hope we sound as good as we look,' Kyle replied.

'Eh, Angus?' He gave his friend a punch on the shoulder and Angus slapped him back.

'OK, guys,' Leo began, flipping back the cover of his notebook. 'Now, first of all I need names. It's Angus Walker, right?'

'And this is Kyle Woodward,' Angus said, gesturing to Kyle and touching his shoulder. 'And our bass guitarist, Liam Smedley.'

'And you are?' Leo asked, turning to Cleo.

'Cleo Greenway,' replied Cleo. 'Spelled K-L-I-O-H.'

'Spelled *how*?' Tansy and Holly chorused.

'Shut it,' Cleo hissed. 'It's my stage name.'

'Hey, don't I know you?' Leo Bellinger, turning to Holly as she tried to suppress her laughter. 'Aren't you Angela Vine's daughter? The campaigning woman?'

'Regrettably, yes.' Holly sighed. 'I hoped you'd forget.'

Leo laughed. 'The funniest story of the decade?' he replied. 'Hardly.'

Five minutes and a lot of speed-writing later . . .

'Great! I think I've got all I need!' Leo flipped his book closed and stuffed his pen into his jacket pocket. 'The pictures and the article will be in tomorrow's paper, OK?'

'Tomorrow? Oh my God . . .' Cleo stammered.

'What's the problem?' Angus asked.

'I never thought it would be tomorrow – I mean, everyone reads the ET and . . .'

'That's the whole idea,' Liam stressed, eyeing her as if she were in immediate need of a brain transplant. 'It's called publicity.'

'And even if we don't make it to the next round, publicity is what the band needs right now,' added Kyle.

'It might,' muttered Cleo under her breath, 'be what you guys need but frankly, I need it like a hole in the head.'

2.00 p.m.

'We can't rehearse now,' Kyle told Cleo as he packed up the band's gear. 'Someone's booked the rehearsal room. So can you make it to Angus's house around seven?'

'Sure,' Cleo told him, not having a clue what excuse she could come up with that would keep her parents off the scent but dead sure that she'd do whatever it took to get closer to Angus.

'Can I come?' Holly burst out. 'You know, as a kind of unbiased observer?'

'I don't know,' Angus began. 'It's a bit off-putting and the room's quite small.'

'Yeah, come, why don't you?' Kyle interrupted. 'It'd be good to run things past someone who hasn't heard it all a thousand times before. Thanks, Holly.'

He wants me there, Holly thought with a thrill. I've connected. Thank you, God.

'Boys, there you are!' Striding across the college forecourt in her scarlet cape and a huge white-fur hat that made her look like a cross between Little Red Riding Hood and a cream meringue was Angus's mother.

'Who's that?' Tansy hissed.

'Mrs Walker,' Holly muttered back. 'She's very in your face.'

'Cleo, angel!' Mrs Walker went on. 'How did it go? Were you all totally splendid?'

'Cleo was a stunner, but then, what's new?' Angus blurted out. Holly couldn't help noticing the way Cleo's face lit up. Or the way Kyle clenched his teeth and looked as if he'd like to wring Angus's neck.

'And Holly – fancy seeing you here,' Mrs Walker went on. 'Quite a little fan club. Well now, all done are you? The car's over there.' She gestured towards a maroon 4x4 parked in the college forecourt. 'Let's get your kit packed away!' She turned to Angus as Liam and Kyle began manhandling the drums towards the car. 'Hurry up, dear. I know you can't bear to wrench yourself away from Cleo, but I have to be at the solicitors' in twenty minutes to sign the contracts.'

Angus turned to Cleo and pecked her on the cheek. 'See you this evening,' he said. 'Don't be late.'

2.05 p.m.
Putting plans on paper

'Cleo, do close your mouth,' Holly urged as the three of them walked across the college quadrangle towards the gates. 'You look like a drowning goldfish.'

'He kissed me,' Cleo breathed.

'Pecked you,' Tansy corrected her. 'Mind you, it's more than some of us get these days.'

'Cold, isn't it?' Holly shivered, desperately trying to change the subject for Tansy's sake.

'I'm going to play it really cool,' Cleo announced, surreptitiously looking from left to right in case her stepfather appeared. 'You know, alluring but calmly serene.'

Holly burst out laughing. 'You weren't exactly calm and serene about the newspaper pictures,' she commented. 'What was all that about? I thought you'd be over the moon.'

'My parents take the evening paper,' Cleo explained. 'If they see the picture, they'll know what's going on and stop it.'

'By the time the paper comes out, the audition will be over,' Holly reasoned, glad that the topic was no longer about relationships.

'But if we win and get to the final, and they've found out about it, I'm dead meat,' Cleo stressed.

'So don't let them see the paper,' Tansy cut in.

'Oh, and like how am I going to manage that?'

Tansy raised her eyes. 'We're delivering the papers, right? You remove the page with the picture before it goes through their letterbox.'

'That's a brilliant idea. Thanks, Tansy. I owe you one.'

'So think up an idea to sort out that jerk Andy!' Holly burst out. 'Sending that photo was just the pits.'

'What photo?' Cleo asked.

'Oh, I forgot, you don't know. Tell her, Tansy. The sooner she knows, the sooner we can work out what to do.'

2.30 p.m.
Tansy's bedroom. Saying it like it is

'OK, how does this sound?' Holly wriggled her bottom into a more comfortable position on Tansy's bed and read the message she had keyed into her phone. 'HOW COULD U B SUCH A SLIME BALL. U R THE PITS, HOLLY.'

'It's a bit strong,' ventured Tansy, nibbling a fingernail.

'It's what he deserves,' Cleo told her. 'How about mine? U DON'T DESERVE TO HAVE A DECENT GIRLFRIEND. WHICH IS Y U'VE CHOSEN SLAG OF THE YEAR. CLEO.'

'Phenomenal!' cried Holly. 'What have you put, Tansy?'

Tansy flushed and dropped her phone into her lap. 'Nothing much, just . . .'

'Come on, we're in this together,' urged Holly, grabbing her phone and scanning the screen. 'Oh.'

'What's she put?' asked Cleo.

Holly didn't have the heart to read it out. She just handed the phone to Cleo and passed the box of tissues to Tansy.

PLEASE DON'T DO THIS 2 ME, Cleo read. I LUV U SO MUCH.

2.45 p.m.
Adding insult to injury. Big time

Tansy's phoned bleeped just as she was seeing Holly and Cleo out of the back door.

'It's from Andy,' she gasped, swallowing hard. She stared at the phone and threw it down on the kitchen table, her eyes filling with tears. I DON'T LOVE U, Cleo read, picking up the phone. SO THERE. She looked at Holly.

'Something very weird is going on,' Holly declared. 'Andy must be on something – it's just not him at all.'

'Get real,' Tansy said. 'You don't have to keep protecting me. He's finished with me and there's nothing I can do about it.'

'That,' declared Cleo, 'is where you are so wrong.'

4.30 p.m.
Planning Paris, over tea and carrot cake

'And then I thought we could take one of the Bateaux Mouches on the River Seine,' Jade's grandmother was saying. 'They're glass-topped boats, darling, and you get a wonderful view of all the sights. Sweetheart, are you homesick?'

'Homesick?' Jade gasped. 'Of course not, Gran. Whatever made you think that?'

'Just the way you keep clutching on to that mobile phone and peering at it every five seconds,' said her grandmother, laughing. 'Or could it be that it's a boy you are pining for?'

'Don't be silly,' Jade protested. 'I don't do boys. I'm not into all that stuff, you know that.'

'Really?' Her gran smiled. 'Right. I see. More cake, darling?'

5.00 p.m.
Lies, damned lies

'Roy, you're home early again. How lovely!' Cleo's mum gave Roy a kiss as he walked through the front door and bit her lip anxiously. 'How was your day?'

'Oh, you know, much the same as usual.' Cleo noticed that he didn't meet her mum's eye but fiddled with his gloves and scarf.

'Did you get the dry cleaning?' her mum asked.

'Sorry, I forgot – I was in a meeting most of the day.'

Tell me about it, thought Cleo, pulling on her boots and unhooking her scarf from the hook. 'Where?' she heard herself ask. 'Where was your meeting?'

'What? Oh – Milton Keynes, the one postponed from yesterday,' he said. 'Been there all day.'

Cleo's stomach lurched. She opened her mouth to tell him he was lying and then shut it again. If she admitted to being at the college, he'd want to know why. And right now her mum was miserable enough without making things worse. But once the audition was over, she was going to have it out with Roy once and for all.

5.10 p.m.
Molecules and mysteries

It was while Holly was finally attempting her science coursework that her phone bleeped.

1 NEW MESSAGE she read, and punched the 'read' button. She saw at once that it was from Andy's phone. KEEP OUT OF IT OR ELSE.

She punched her phone and rang Cleo's number. 'Cleo, listen, I've had a text from Andy,' she began and then read it out, emphasising each word.

'That does it,' said Cleo. 'I'm just off to do the papers with Tansy, and I'm going to have it out with him. What's more, I'm sending my text off to him right now.'

'I thought you did that this afternoon when I sent mine,' Holly replied.

'To be honest,' Cleo admitted, 'I bottled out. But now . . .'

'OK, do it,' Holly urged. 'And let me know how you get on tonight, OK? And don't hold back!'

6.10 p.m.
Explanations – or excuses?

'Tansy, don't you dare chicken out now,' Cleo warned as they walked up the path to Andy's front door. 'Just look him in the eye and watch him squirm.'

She rang the doorbell. Within seconds, Andy's mother answered it, one of the twins in her arms. 'Tansy! Oh, the paper – thank you so much, I was waiting for that.' She almost snatched it from Tansy's grasp.

'Is everything OK?' Tansy ventured.

'OK? Of course it is – oh, I expect you're wondering what was going on when you called this morning,' Mrs Richards gabbled. 'Well, I can explain all that. We had intruders in our back garden last night, and one of the neighbours spotted them and called the police. Very Neighbourhood Watch!' She laughed nervously. 'I'd better go – Clover needs a nappy change.'

'Could we speak to Andy, please?' Cleo interjected firmly as Mrs Richards attempted to shut the front door. 'It's very important.'

'Andy? Oh, sorry, no – he's out. Besides, I'm not sure it's a good idea. . .'

'Why? What has he said?' Tansy panicked.

'I wasn't going to say anything,' Mrs Richards said, hitching the baby higher on her hip. 'I've always tried not to interfere – but after the state Andy got into at the weekend and all the trouble it caused . . . well, I just feel you could have done a bit more to stop it happening.'

'What state? Stopped what happening?' Tansy frowned. 'I didn't see Andy this weekend.'

'Come on, now, there's no need to pretend,' Mrs Richards protested.

'I'm not!' Tansy protested. 'I don't even know what you're talking about.'

Andy's mother looked confused. 'I just assumed that you two had been together on Saturday night . . .'

'Did he say that?' Cleo cut in.

'No, but then again, he was totally out of it, throwing up all over the place. I thought you must have had a few drinks and it got out of hand.'

'I don't drink and neither does he – well, only a shandy occasionally,' Tansy said. 'And on Saturday, I was stuck at home watching TV.'

'Sorry, love,' Mrs Richards murmured. 'Perhaps I jumped to conclusions.' She bit her lip. 'Andy isn't exactly communicating with me much at the moment,' she said.

'You and me both,' muttered Tansy.

'Do you know when he'll be back?' Cleo asked, reaching out to tickle the baby.

'Not sure – he's having a day out with his father and Ricky. They've gone quad biking. I ask you – in this weather! Still, it's a bit of male bonding!' She gave another shaky laugh, and jigged the baby up and down on her hip. 'They won't be back till late, but you could always give him a call – oh no, of course, you can't.'

'We could,' Tansy said eagerly.

Andy's mum shook her head. 'He's lost his phone. Honestly, he'd mislay his head if it wasn't screwed on to his neck.'

'Lost it?' Cleo's mouth dropped open and she prodded Tansy surreptitiously in the back. 'When?'

'Goodness knows.' Andy's mother shrugged. 'He only told me about it over breakfast this morning, and then he had the cheek to ask me to fork out the cash for a new one!'

'Do you know where he lost it?' Cleo asked. 'I mean – we'll keep an eye out for it.'

'Haven't a clue,' his mother said. 'You think he tells me anything? I'm just his mother. Look, I've got to go.'

'You'll tell Andy I called round?' Tansy pleaded.

'Sure,' his mother said. 'And Tansy? I'm sorry. I'm just in a bit of state right now.'

Post-mortem

'You know what this means, don't you?' Cleo demanded two seconds later. 'If Andy lost his phone, he couldn't have sent you those messages.'

'Sure he could,' Tansy retorted. 'Before he lost it.'

'Yes.' Cleo nodded patiently. 'But when did the last couple come through? Earlier today, right?'

'So?'

'So his mum said he told her this morning that he'd lost it, and wanted a new one,' Cleo said triumphantly.

Tansy's eyes widened. 'You mean . . .?' she began.

'What I mean is that someone else has been setting you up. And I've a pretty good idea who it is.'

6.45 p.m.

'That is one cool idea,' Holly said on the phone later. 'So when do we set the trap?'

'First thing tomorrow morning,' Cleo said. 'If we leave

it till then, there's less chance of anyone sussing what's going on. Now, you know what you've got to do?'

7.45 p.m.
Band banter

'OK, that's it!' Kyle declared as Cleo hit the final note of her song for the fourth time. 'We've never been this good – don't let's push our luck!'

'Was I OK?' Cleo asked, and Holly had to hide a smile as she watched the way Cleo tilted her hips and edged towards Angus.

'Stunning,' Angus assured her. 'Come on. Let's go and get something to drink. I'm parched.'

'I've got to go,' Kyle said as they climbed the stairs from the basement to the kitchen.

'Go?' Holly asked. 'Do you have to?'

'Sadly, yes,' he said, nodding. 'I'm already three days late with my essay and my tutor is about to have apoplexy!'

Just my luck, thought Holly to herself. I get to be within a metre of him and then discover he's a work freak.

'See you in the morning,' Angus said. 'Don't be late.'

'Stop fretting,' Kyle retorted. 'I'll be there. Nine on the dot.'

'It's eight-thirty,' Angus pointed out.

'Whatever,' Kyle said, shrugging.

'Look, if you're not going to take this seriously . . .' Angus began.

'I'm just winding you up,' Kyle laughed, and punched him lightly on the arm. 'Chill, man, for God's sake.'

It seemed to Holly that Angus looked far more wounded than the conversation deserved. She didn't want to believe it, but just possibly Jade might have had a point.

Ten minutes later . . .

'When again, clearly not. She and Cleo had been about to leave when Angus's mum came running downstairs.

'Holly dear, how nice to see you again! And Cleo – my goodness, your voice! I could hear you from the spare room – what control!'

Angus slipped an arm round Cleo's shoulder. 'She is something rather special, isn't she?' He smiled. 'Biggest asset the band's got, if you ask me.' He gave Cleo a squeeze and brushed his lips past her left ear. Holly thought Cleo was about to pass out with delight.

'Well, of course, Gus, we all know how *you* feel about her,' his mother chortled. 'Now we just have to hope the judges feel the same.'

'She knows?' Cleo hissed as Mrs Walker hurried into the kitchen. 'I thought we said we'd keep it quiet.'

'I couldn't keep it a secret for ever,' he rejoined. 'She opened the letter confirming the time and date – I had to come clean.'

'She opens your post?' Holly burst out.

'It was an accident,' Angus replied hastily, turning back to Cleo. 'Anyway, no harm done. She's hardly likely to meet your mother, is she? And by the time she does, it will all be over. Stop fretting.'

Now where have I heard that phrase before? Holly thought.

WEDNESDAY

6.30 a.m.
The Cedars. Panic stations

'Holly – wake up!' Her mother burst into the bedroom, switched on the light and shook Holly violently.

'Whasematter?' Holly opened one eye. 'Mum, go away – I'm sleeping.'

'No, you're not!' Her mother ripped the duvet off the bed. 'It's Serena – she's been rushed to hospital.'

'What? Oh my God, what's wrong?' Holly sat bolt upright in bed.

'It seems she's pregnant again,' her mother said, pulling back the curtains. 'They hadn't told anyone because they wanted to wait till she was a few months gone – you know, with what happened before.' Holly's sister-in-law had had two miscarriages since the birth of William, both at sixteen weeks.

'She's not losing this one, is she?' Holly gasped.

'I pray she's not,' her mum replied. 'But it doesn't look too good. Come on – we need to leave for Leicester at once. We're picking William up from the childminder and bringing him back here.'

'When you say "we"?'

'You and me,' her mother replied. 'And get a move on – it snowed overnight and the roads will be dreadful.'

'Can't Dad go?' Holly dreaded her mother's driving at the best of times, let alone in bad weather and a panic.

'Oh, get real. We've got this dinner tonight and he still

76

hasn't finished his speech. Which reminds me, you'll have to stay in this evening to babysit Wills.'

'But I've made plans,' Holly protested.

'So unmake them,' her mother retorted. 'Family comes first. Now get dressed.'

7.30 a.m.
Giving thanks for a gullible mother

It was as Cleo was spooning yogurt down her throat with one eye on the clock that she realised her mother would be expecting her home from the paper round by nine o'clock. In all her careful planning and deception, it was the one vital fact she had missed. She was running a few excuses across her brain when her mother shuffled into the kitchen in her housecoat and mules.

'Tea, Mum?' Cleo smiled, because softening up mothers was crucial when you were on the back foot.

Her mother shook her head. 'Black coffee,' she said with a sigh, reaching up to the kitchen cupboard and taking down a bottle of painkillers. 'I've got a killer of a headache.'

'Coffee will only make you feel worse,' Cleo reminded her sternly.

'I couldn't feel worse,' her mother retaliated, stubbornly spooning Nescafé into a mug. She turned to Cleo. 'Tell me honestly,' she begged. 'Do I look my age?'

No, thought Cleo. Right now you look sixty-five and climbing.

'Of course not,' she assured her. 'Oh, and Mum – I won't be back till this afternoon. I'm going straight to the library to crack on with my history essay.' She held her breath, crossed her fingers behind her back and prayed.

'That's good,' her mother nodded. 'Lettie's going to the stables all day so I can go back to bed.'

Cleo wanted to tell her that moping about was not helping anyone but having been let off the hook so easily, she wasn't about to push her luck. 'I'm off,' she told her mother, wriggling of the bar stool and giving her a quick hug. 'See you later. And cheer up.'

'What,' her mother said, sighing, 'is there to be cheerful about?' She peered at Cleo. 'Darling, aren't you a little overdressed for a paper round?'

7.50 a.m.
Rallying the troops

HOPE PARIS IS FUN. CAN U TEXT ANDY'S PHONE AND SAY YOU CAN'T W8 2 C HIM AND TANSY 2NITE? ASK WOT TIME. XPLAIN L8R. DO IT 4 T. CLEO.

Jade reread Cleo's message for the third time as she and her gran waited to board the Eurostar train at Ashford station. She still couldn't get her head round it. But if what Cleo was saying would help Tansy, she'd do it. At least she wasn't going to be round to pick up the pieces.

CAN'T W8 2 C U AND T 2NITE. WOT TIME? JADE.

She zapped the message to Andy's phone and pressed the off button. And then switched it on again. Just in case anyone was trying to get in touch with her. Not that they would. But just in case.

8.00 a.m.

'I've got to dash,' Cleo told Tansy the moment they had fetched the papers from Mrs Patel. 'I'm due at the theatre in half an hour. Now, you know what you've got to do?'

Tansy nodded. 'Send a text to Andy's phone saying I'll see him tonight,' she said.

'But don't say where you're going, right?' Cleo urged. 'That's Holly's job'

'What if I see Andy this morning?' Tansy queried.

'At eight o'clock? Get real,' Cleo said, laughing. 'You said yourself he never surfaces before ten. And don't go asking for him, promise me?'

'OK,' Tansy nodded reluctantly. 'Whatever. Good luck.'

'You too,' Cleo replied. 'Don't worry – today's the day Melanie Hankinson gets what she deserves.'

8.10 a.m.
Bad news – and how!

Tansy hovered on the doorstep of Andy's house. She knew Cleo had told her not to ring the bell, but just dumping the paper and walking away seemed like such a missed opportunity. Not that she wanted to look like she was hassling him. But then again, she didn't want him to think she had given up on him.

'No,' she told herself firmly out loud. 'Just send the text message and leave it at that.'

GR8 TO C U YESTERDAY. WERE U HOT OR WOT? C U 2NITE. BYE SEXY! T.

She offered up a silent prayer and zapped the message

across to Andy. Well, to Melanie, if Cleo's hunch was right.

She had just turned to go down the path and carry on with her paper round, when the front door opened. She spun round. Andy's dad, briefcase in hand, slammed the door behind him and smiled at her.

'Hiya, Tansy,' he said. 'Perfect timing – I can't do without a paper to read on the bus.'

Tansy had to bite her tongue to stop her from asking about Andy. 'What have you done to your face, Mr Richards?' she asked, eyeing a nasty cut and purple bruise on his cheek.

'Oh, that happened yesterday,' he said with a laugh. 'Sorry you couldn't come with us. Mind you, I guess quad biking isn't a girly thing, especially in this weather. Andy wasn't surprised when you said no.'

'I didn't – he never . . .' Tansy spluttered, then stopped. Andy hadn't invited her which meant only one thing. He didn't want her around. So whether Melanie was sending those messages or not, it didn't really matter. The bottom line was that Andy didn't want her anywhere near him.

8.15 a.m.
Somewhere on the M1 in a traffic jam

'Mum, please,' Holly pleaded for the third time. 'You just don't get it.'

'Holly, I get it perfectly,' her mother retorted, drumming her fingers on the steering wheel. 'Just because you can't have yet another evening out with your friends, you're throwing a strop. You are so selfish.'

'That's the whole point, I'm not being selfish,' Holly stressed. 'I love babysitting Wills, you know that. It's just that Tansy's had some terrible news . . .'

'Tansy? I was talking to her mother yesterday and she didn't say anything about bad news.'

'It's not the kind of bad news you share with your mother,' Holly stressed. 'It's Andy – he's dumped her. Except that he probably hasn't. If I tell you the whole story, will you promise to listen and not interrupt till I've finished?'

'Of course, why do you need to ask?'

'Because I know you,' said Holly. 'This is what's happened . . .'

It took five minutes and countless interruptions to get the message across to her mother, but at the end she saw the glimmer of a smile flit across her mother's face.

'It's certainly an original idea,' she said, slipping the car into second gear as the traffic finally started moving. 'But I have to go to this dinner with your father – it's his presidential night after all.'

'Well, can't you get a babysitter?' Holly begged. 'Mrs Morton – she'd do it.'

Mrs Morton, who had been Holly's babysitter when she was little, lived a few streets away from The Cedars in a retirement flat full of china frogs and pictures of her late husband.

'Oh, I don't know.' Her mother sighed. 'It's such a responsibility. I mean, I can't leave William with just anyone.'

'You left me with Mrs M,' Holly pointed out. 'And I survived.'

'I'll think about it,' her mother conceded.

For once, Holly didn't press the point. There was too much at stake to risk pushing her luck.

10.00 a.m.
In the spotlight

I am going to die. Or throw up. Or cry.

Cleo gripped the mike in her right hand and stared out into the auditorium. A load of guys from the TV company were sitting halfway back, all with clipboards and intense expressions. Behind them, clusters of other contestants perched on seats or wandered along the aisles.

'OK, guys,' called one of the men. 'In your own time. And your number is called?'

'"Don't Leave Me Lonely,"' Angus called back.

'Oh – that one.' The producer sounded bored.

'I said we should have written our own stuff,' Liam hissed.

'Too late now,' Angus snapped back. 'Cleo, just give it all you've got, OK?'

'Quiet please!' one of the TV crew shouted and the auditorium fell silent. The lights dimmed and the band struck up the intro.

'You said you were going and my heart began to break . . .'

Cleo could hear the shake in her voice. Get a grip, she told herself. This is your one chance. Go for it.

'I looked into your eyes and saw our love was fake . . .'

Better, she thought. Think of Tansy. Think of all the emotion.

'Saw your deception, your twisted little smile . . .'

She caught sight of someone in the audience moving their body in time to the beat. I can do this, she told herself. I can do it good.

'Don't leave me lonely, lo-oh-ohnly . . . Don't leave me lonely again!'

10.15 a.m.
Tantrum-avoidance techniques

'Go see Mummy now?' William asked, clutching on to Holly's hand as she strapped him into his car seat.

'Not now, darling,' her mother cut in. 'You're coming home with Grandma and Holly. Won't that be nice?'

'Want to see Mummy.' His lower lip quivered, and he took a deep breath. Holly knew from experience what would happen next.

'I know what,' she said enthusiastically. 'Let's go to Grandma's and draw a big picture for Mummy. And then we can take it to her later on.'

William eyed her suspiciously and held his breath.

'And we can make snowballs. And cookies,' she improvised hastily as she noticed that the muscles in his legs tensed, ready to embark on one of his famous tantrums.

'Wiv chocolate buttons?' William queried.

'Of course,' said Holly.

'And wellow icing and kleppies?'

'With anything you want,' Holly assured him.

'OK then.' He smiled one of his angelic, butter-wouldn't-melt-in-his-mouth smiles and stuck his thumb in his mouth.

'Well done, darling,' her mother said approvingly. 'You've got a knack.'

'One problem,' said Holly. 'What on earth are kleppies?'

'Search me,' her mother said, smiling, 'but I'm sure you'll find out soon enough.'

10.30 a.m.
Heading home

'And the big bad wolf said, "I'll huff and I'll puff and I'll blow" – oh, flip and sugarplum fairies!'

'That's a new version of the story,' commented Holly's mother, pulling out to overtake an elderly Ford Fiesta. 'What's the matter?'

'I forget to send a message to Andy's phone,' she said. 'Cleo will kill me.' She pulled her phone from the back pocket of her jeans.

'I thought you weren't speaking to Andy,' her mother said.

'Mum,' Holly said, sighing, 'I told you. It's Andy's phone, but not Andy, right? We think it's this other girl, and when she gets all these messages that she thinks are meant for Andy, but are really meant to trap her . . .'

'I get the gist,' her mother said. 'Just do it and get back to the story, will you? William's going a very funny shade of green.'

GR8 IDEA ABOUT MTG AT FUNKIE JUNKIE'S. C U THERE AT 8. HOLLY.

'That should set things going,' she murmured, slipping her phone back into the pocket. 'Right, William where was I? I'll huff and I'll – oh no! Mum! William's thrown up all over my jeans.'

8 4

12.00 noon
La vie Parisienne

'I can't believe we're here,' Jade said, as the taxi drove them from the Gare du Nord to their hotel. 'Can we go to the Eiffel Tower? And Notre Dame? And I really want to see the Louvre museum and the streets where the barricades were in the Revolution, like in *Les Misérables* and . . .'

'Steady on!' her grandmother said with a laugh, clasping a hand to her chest. 'You're making me exhausted just listening to you. We'll do it all, I promise. But first, we'll go to the hotel and have lunch. Something uniquely French.' She winked at Jade. 'What's it to be? Snails or frogs' legs?'

'Oh, Gran, be serious,' Jade shuddered. 'I couldn't possibly . . .' She paused as her phone bleeped.

BIENVENUE A PARIS! SORRY, THAT'S THE LIMIT OF MY FRENCH. HAVE A COOL TRIP. FLYNN. XX

'Oh wow, it works over here! Brilliant!' Jade couldn't help a broad grin spreading across her face. 'He said it might.'

'Aha!' Her grandmother laughed. 'He? But darling, you don't have boyfriends, remember?'

'He's not a boyfriend,' Jade stressed. 'Just a guy I met on the train coming down yesterday. He's in a wheelchair and I helped him, that's all.'

'Really? You could have fooled me. But then again, what do I know? Now as I was saying – frogs' legs or escargots?'

12.45 p.m.

2NITE IS OFF. ANDY.

Holly read the message on her phone and laughed. 'Oh is it, Melanie Hankinson? In your dreams, sunshine!'

1.00 p.m.
Crunch time

'This is it!' Angus chewed his lip as a couple of the TV team climbed up on to the stage to announce which bands had been selected. 'I guess we blew it – some of the other bands were well better than us.'

'Why do you always have to look on the down side of everything?' Kyle retorted. 'Cleo was loads better than that guy with Posturing Pig.'

'Yeah,' said Angus, 'but Spontaneous Combustion's drummer was amazing.'

'Sssh!' Cleo hissed. 'They're starting.'

One of the TV producers stepped forward and tapped the mike. 'OK, guys,' he said. 'I guess you're all desperate to know who's going forward to the big night on Saturday. We could only select three bands and they are . . .' He paused and glanced at his clipboard. 'Spontaneous Combustion.'

There was a burst of applause and shrieks of joy from the three guys that made up the band.

'Told you,' groaned Angus, his chin dropping onto his chest.

'Maximum Penalty . . .' the TV producer continued.

'They weren't that brilliant,' Kyle said, frowning.

'The bass guitarist was rubbish.'

Cleo realised she was holding her breath. Only one more band could qualify and if it wasn't them . . .

'And last but by no means least – it's KickStart.'

'We did it!' Cleo shrieked, jumping up and down and clapping her hands. 'We did it!'

Before she realised what she was doing, she had flung her arms round Angus' neck and kissed his cheek. He flushed bright red and then kissed Cleo nervously on the neck.

'Man, we're in!' Kyle cried, punching the air. 'Yes!'

'If the winning bands will come backstage, we'll give you the details for Saturday's final selection at Rock Hard,' the producer was saying. 'Bad luck the rest of you.'

Two seconds later . . .

'So,' the producer said, 'you all understand the rules for Saturday? Everyone attending Rock Hard gets a vote, so pack in your fans! Oh, and remember, you have to play a different number from the one you used today.'

Angus pulled a face. 'I guess it's down to you,' he whispered in Cleo's ear. 'We'll have to choose something you can sing. Do you know any really new cutting edge stuff?'

'How new?' Cleo asked, a thought whizzing into her mind.

'Newer the better,' he muttered. 'It would be a disaster to find we were singing something that one of the others had chosen.'

'Actually,' Cleo said with a broad grin, 'I think I can guarantee that won't happen. What are you doing for the next two days?'

1.20 p.m.
In the street – but who cares?

'And now I've changed, directions rearranged, so don't hang around no-oh-more / Don't come back, I'm right on track and I don't want to hear about you-ooooo / Cos I've changed my direction too!'

Cleo held the top C as long as she could, conscious that passers-by were eyeing her with a mixture of amusement and surprise.

'That's good.' Kyle nodded approvingly.

'Cool,' Liam agreed.

'No probs,' Angus cut in enthusiastically, scanning the restaurant for a free table. 'Come round tonight, why don't you? About seven?'

'Great.' Cleo nodded eagerly again, over the moon at the thought of a few hours on her own with Angus. 'Now can we eat? I'm starving.'

1.30 p.m. (2.30 p.m. in France)

'They taste just like chicken,' Jade commented after her grandmother insisted that she tasted one of her frog's legs. 'But I'll stick with my cheese on toast . . .'

'*Croque monsieur*,' her gran corrected her. 'When in France, speak like the French do. What's that awful racket?'

'Sorry, my phone – I forgot to switch it off,' Jade apologised, grabbing it from her bag.

2NITE CANCELLED. ANDY.

Jade shrugged. It didn't matter to her one way or the other, but she couldn't help thinking that Tansy would be dead stressy.

'Another message from this non-boyfriend, darling?' her gran asked good humouredly.

'No, just a mate,' Jade replied and found herself wondering why she felt disappointed.

1.45 p.m.
Line management

'The phone!' Holly's mum cried, dumping a black bag of rubbish in the middle of the hall. 'It'll be Richard – oh goodness!' She snatched the phone. 'Yes, Richard? Oh it's you, Tansy. Yes, Holly's here.' She thrust the phone into Holly's hand. 'And be quick,' she hissed. 'I want the line kept free in case your brother phones.'

'Hi, Tansy,' Holly said, waving her mother away. 'What's up?'

'Can you talk?'

'Sort of,' Holly said, using the code for 'My mother is within earshot'.

'I get it,' said Tansy. 'Well, just listen and say yes and no. I've had a message from – well, if you're right, from Melanie.'

'Me too.'

'Saying that tonight's off?'

'Exactly,' Holly affirmed.

'Mine says U AND ME JUST DON'T WORK. 2NITE'S OFF. ANDY. That proves she's trying to split Andy and me up, right?'

'Precisely.' One-word conversations were so frustrating.

'So do you think Melanie's putting us off because she thinks Andy will turn up at Funkie Junkie's and she can have him all to herself?'

'Got it in one.' Holly nodded.

'When we get there, I'm going to kill her,' Tansy declared. 'Not that there's much point, but she's obviously decided she wants him and . . .'

'Tansy, that's it! It all makes sense! The weekend . . . what his mum said . . . hang on, I'll call you back.'

Two seconds later . . .

'And where do you think you're going?' Holly's mum looked up from the floor where she was building a Lego castle with William. 'You said you'd play with Wills while I sorted out my clothes for tonight.'

'About tonight,' Holly began, her hand on the door. 'If I play with William all afternoon, and get his tea and bath him . . .'

'Mrs Morton is coming at seven-thirty,' her mother said, smiling. 'But you must be back by ten on the dot – she's old and she gets tired and . . .'

Holly sped across the room and flung her arms round her mother's neck. 'Mum, you're an angel,' she cried, kissing her cheek. 'Thank you, thank you, thank you – and I won't ask for any other favours for weeks, I promise.'

'If I believed that, darling, I really would need my brain tested.'

And then . . .

Holly was about to ring Tansy when her phone shrilled.

'We did it, we did it!' Cleo shrieked. 'We're in the final. I can't stop shaking, I'm so excited. We're just going for pizzas to celebrate.'

'Brilliant,' Holly enthused. 'That is so cool.'

'Listen, you haven't forgotten about dumping the newspapers tonight, have you?' Cleo urged. 'I don't deliver to Weston Way, so there's nothing I can do about it.'

'Sure,' Holly agreed. 'And hey, I think I've sussed something you should know about.'

'What?'

'Don't say anything to Tansy yet – she's in a state as it is. Remember you told me that Andy's mum said he'd stormed out on Saturday night?'

'Yeah, so what?'

'I think he was with Melanie,' Holly declared.

'Oh, Holly, get real!'

'Listen!' Holly insisted. 'He'd been invited to Ella's party right? Melanie is Ella's sister. So she'd have been there.'

'And you think . . .'

'That Melanie tried to get off with Andy,' Holly finished. 'And just maybe . . .'

'What the hell? I've got to go.'

'Cleo, wait. I might be wrong but . . .'

The phone went dead. And I, thought Holly with a sigh, am supposed to be the one who overreacts.

2.05 p.m.
Pizza? Forget it!

Cleo stuffed the phone into her bag and stared across the road, the colour draining from her face.

'What's the matter?' Angus queried. 'What are you gawping at?' He followed her gaze. 'Wow,' he breathed.

'Now that is one cool car.' He gestured approvingly towards the bright yellow Lotus Elan which had pulled up at the kerb. 'Into cars, are you?' Angus queried.

'Come on, you two!' Liam called from the doorway of Pizza Express. 'There's only one table left.'

Cleo dragged her gaze away and reluctantly followed Angus. She didn't bother telling him that it wasn't a question of her being into cars. It was more the worry of who she had seen getting into that swanky sports model.

It was her stepdad. And the driver was the woman from the college. The woman on whose cheek Roy had just planted a very enthusiastic kiss.

4.05 p.m.
Kleppy hunting

'Kleppies! Gotta have kleppies!'

Holly counted to ten as William screeched his demand for the fourth time. 'We've got chocolate buttons, and sprinkles and these lovely silver stars,' she coaxed.

'Get kleppies!'

If this was child rearing, thought Holly, she thought she might remain celibate for life.

'Red kleppies!' William screamed, banging his little fists up and down on the table and sending bits of cake mixture in all directions.

'So kleppies are red, are they?' Holly asked him. 'Right – what's red and goes in cakes? Oh – you mean cherries!'

'Yes, that's right!' William looked triumphant. 'Kleppies!'

'We haven't got any kleppies – I mean, cherries,' Holly

told him. 'So why don't we – no, William, don't start yelling again, please.'

'Holly, can't you keep William quiet?' her father thundered, poking his head round the kitchen door. 'I'm trying to practise my speech and – oh, for pity's sake!' The lights spluttered and died. 'Not another confounded power cut!' he stormed. 'Honestly you'd think we were living in Siberia.'

'Light gone,' William observed. 'Dark.' His lower lip trembled. 'Light come back now?' he asked hopefully.

'No, William, not yet,' Holly's father informed him. 'There's a power cut. It's because someone somewhere has probably cut through a power cable.'

'Dad,' interrupted Holly, 'He's only three years old.'

'One is never too young to learn basic science,' countered her father. 'Now where are the candles?'

'You can't burn candles with William around,' Holly reasoned. 'One is never too old to learn basic Safety First.'

4.10 p.m.
Bad hair moment

'I don't believe this!' Holly's mother said, standing at the top of the stairs in her bathrobe, her grey hair dripping wet. 'Of all the times to have a power cut.'

'Just towel it dry and then tong it when the power comes back,' Holly advised. 'It'll be fine.'

'Fine it will not be!' Holly's father commented, emerging from the study. 'I've just phoned East Midlands Electricity and guess what? I was right – severed cable and it'll take several hours to restore power.'

'I'm going to look a mess for the dinner,' her mother wailed.

'No you won't,' Holly replied soothingly. 'The unstructured look is very in these days.'

'Cook cakes now,' William asked hopefully.

'No, darling,' Holly told him. 'The oven's broken for a bit. No William, don't cry – let's play a game . . .'

'Go get sweeties?' William was clearly in a bargaining mood. 'No cry, get sweeties.'

'And while you're at it, get some more torch batteries from the corner shop,' her mother cut in. 'Your father's let them all run down.'

'Don't blame me,' Mr Vine retorted. 'You wanted the attic cleared and the light up there kept flickering – I couldn't see a thing. I had to use the torches.'

'Switching them off when you'd finished might have been a good idea,' his wife snapped back. 'And leaving boxes in the middle of the landing is hardly sensible – I could have broken my ankle.'

'Come on, Wills. Let's put your coat and welly boots on and we'll go to the shop. Granny and Grandpa are about to say naughty words to each other.'

4.30 p.m.
Hot brush and gossip

Holly's mother was about to ring the fifth hairdresser in the *Yellow Pages* when the lights came on. The phone rang just as she plugged in the hot brush.

'Angela, it's Clarity. Listen, I've spoken to Val Richards. I called in on my way back from the shops.'

'And?'

'She says the police were there because the neighbours had a break-in.'

'Oh, well, that's OK then,' Holly's mum replied. 'To be honest, I was worried because I haven't heard a word from Val in two weeks.'

'Actually, it's not OK,' Mrs Meadows stressed. 'She's changed her story – she told Tansy the police came because the neighbours had seen intruders in Val's back garden.'

'Maybe she was in a stress and got muddled?'

'She was in a stress all right, and if you ask me it had nothing to do with burglars. I think she was lying through her back teeth. I swear I heard shouting when I rang the doorbell. And she'd definitely been crying.' Clarity sighed. 'She didn't even invite me in for a cup of coffee.'

'That's not like her,' Mrs Vine admitted. 'Usually you have to go in and coo over the babies.'

'What do you think we should do? I mean, if something's wrong, shouldn't we be offering to help?' Clarity suggested.

Not now, thought Holly's mum. Hair first, charity later. 'Look, I'm in a mad dash right now – can I call you tomorrow? Then we can work out a plan of action.'

'But . . .'

'Bye, Clarity!'

4.31 p.m.
Face to face with the culprit

'William, you can't have all those sweets,' Holly said firmly. 'Which is it to be – chocolate buttons or jelly tots?'

'Telly jots,' William said decisively.

'Right,' she replied, grabbing a bag. 'Now, we'll get Grandpa's batteries and then go home.' She stopped dead as she caught sight of a familiar figure, peering short-sightedly at the rack of batteries. It was Andy. 'So you are still alive?' she said sarcastically touching him on the shoulder.

He jumped and wheeled round. 'What? Oh, Holly. Hi.' He coloured visibly and grabbed a handful of batteries. 'We've got a power cut,' he began.

'Yes, so have we,' Holly cut in, reaching out for a bumper pack and following him to the checkout. 'Found your phone yet, have you?'

'How did you know I'd lost it?' he gasped.

'Your mum told Tansy,' she returned, thankful that there was a long queue and he couldn't get away. 'You remember Tansy? Your *girlfriend*? The one you treat like dirt!'

'I don't, I haven't spoken to her . . .'

'For days,' concluded Holly. 'Precisely. Why? Because of Melanie Hankinson, perhaps?' She wasn't sure what reaction she had expected but it certainly wasn't the look of horror and fear that crossed his face.

'Melanie? You've been talking to Melanie?'

'Holly open sweeties now!' William tugged at her

hand. She knew her mother would be furious if she let him eat before his tea, but she needed him to keep quiet, so she ripped the packet open with her teeth and thrust them into his eager little hand.

'And what if I *have* been talking to Melanie?' she asked as the queue edged forward. 'Got something to hide, have you?'

'No, I ?' he stammered. 'I mean, it didn't happen.'

'What didn't?'

Andy swallowed hard. 'Nothing,' he mumbled. 'I mean, whatever she's saying, it's not true.'

'So what's with the hateful messages you've been sending Tansy,' Holly demanded, convinced he was hiding something.

'What messages?'

'Telling Tansy you were dumping her, saying you didn't want her hassling you . . .' She paused and held his gaze. 'Sending her a photo of Melanie – that was so sick!'

'A picture? That is so not true!' Andy exploded, hurling the batteries onto the checkout desk. 'How could I send anything when I've lost my phone?'

'Right,' Holly declared, aware that time was running out. 'So let's have the full story. From the beginning. Like now.'

Five minutes later . . .

'You have to believe me!' Andy urged as he finished telling Holly what had happened. 'Not that you will – girls always want to think the worst about guys.'

'Go home now!' William interrupted, tugging on Holly's hand. 'Now!'

'Be quiet, William!' Holly snapped, shivering in the icy wind and stamping her feet to keep warm. William wailed, so Holly stuffed another sweet into his mouth. 'Actually, I think I do believe you,' she told Andy. 'But it still doesn't explain why you've blown Tansy out.'

Andy swallowed hard and looked away. 'I haven't,' he murmured. 'There's a whole load of stuff going on, that's all.'

'With Melanie, I suppose?'

'No!' he shouted. 'Just – stuff. OK, so I did some dumb things but . . .'

'You really want it to work out with Tansy?' Holly demanded. 'What would you do to make sure it turned out right?'

'Anything,' replied Andy. 'Whatever it took.'

'Right,' said Holly 'So this is what you do.'

Meanwhile . . .

'I look quite cool, don't I?' Cleo pointed admiringly to the picture in the paper as she and Tansy stood on the corner of Weston Way. 'Even my thighs look kind of smaller than usual,' she mused.

'Come on,' Tansy said, shivering. 'I'm getting cold. How many copies have we got to doctor?'

'Mine, yours, both sets of neighbours in case they spill the beans – that should do it. It's a good thing the picture's on the middle page – we can slip it out and no one will notice.'

Tansy wasn't convinced, but said nothing.

'Sorted.' Cleo beamed, chucking the unwanted pages into the waste bin by the bus shelter.

'Can we get on now, please?' asked Tansy. 'I need to wash my hair and do my eyebrows before we go to Funkie Junkie's.'

'Oh, I forgot to tell you,' Cleo cut in. 'I can't come. Angus wants me to practise my new song for Saturday. There's load to get sorted.'

'Oh, and sorting out me suddenly takes a back seat, does it?' snapped Tansy. 'Well thanks very much.'

'Don't be like that,' pleaded Cleo. 'You've got Holly. And besides, it was your idea that Angus helped me with the music, remember?'

'I suppose,' Tansy muttered grudgingly. 'But what if Melanie's there tonight with a whole bunch of her mates? Them against us two?'

'Oh, stop being so dramatic,' cried Cleo, who was feeling guilty enough as it was. 'Holly's match enough for anyone. It'll be fine. Trust me.'

'I did,' Tansy said with a sigh. 'Remember?'

5.00 p.m.

'Holly, is that you?' Holly's mum shouted from the kitchen.

Holly grabbed the *Evening Telegraph* and began thumbing through the pages. 'Yes, I'm back,' she called. 'Go and say hi to Granny, William.'

She pushed William towards the kitchen door. She had just managed to slip the centre section from the paper and stuff it inside her fleece when her mother stuck her head round the door.

'And just where have you been?' her mother demanded, blowing out two candles as William eyed them in fascination, and snatching the batteries from Holly's hand. 'I was worried sick. It doesn't take half an hour to buy a few batteries. Not that I need them now, the lights are back on, but all the same . . .'

'Sorry, Mum, but I met Andy.'

'I don't really care if you came face to face with the Prime Minister,' her mother exploded, chucking the batteries into a drawer. 'You know I have to go out and Wills has to have his bath and . . . oh. Andy.'

'Yes.' Holly nodded, flinging the paper onto a vacant chair. 'And we had a chat.'

'Have you sorted it all out?' her mother asked.

'Ask me again tomorrow morning. And hopefully the answer will be yes.'

5.45 p.m.

'. . . and then she says she's not coming because of this dumb competition,' Tansy moaned. 'That's why I came over. I thought we'd go together because no way am I going to Funkie J's on my own. It's all down to you and me.'

'Not quite,' Holly said with a smile, blowing out a couple of tea lights on her dressing table.

'Leave the others, they look pretty,' Tansy said. 'What do you mean – not quite?'

'I saw Andy today,' Holly confessed. 'He did go to Ella's party but . . .?'

'The pig! How could he?' Tansy burst out.

'Listen!' ordered Holly. 'He had a row with his parents, stormed out of the house and then realised it was freezing cold and he hadn't even got a coat. Then he remembered Ella's party was going on round the corner.'

'Oh, very convenient,' snapped Tansy. 'And you fell for that story?'

'Actually, I think that bit is true,' Holly assured her friend. 'He looked so miserable especially when he said what Melanie was accusing him of doing.'

'Which was?'

'This is the bit you're not going to like,' Holly warned her. 'Melanie says that Andy snogged her senseless and told her – well, a few things.' She paused.

'Like what?' Tansy's voice was tight with pent-up emotion.

'That he would chuck you and go out with her,' Holly gabbled. 'But listen ?' she put her hand over Tansy's mouth to stop her exploding in a stream of invective '? he says he can't remember anything about the party. Apparently he got drunk.'

Tansy pulled Holly's hand away from her mouth. 'Oh, and got amnesia as a result? Hardly!' Tears began trickling down Tansy's cheeks and she brushed them away angrily.

'Andy says he can't stand Melanie and that he wouldn't ask her out if she was the last female on the planet,' Holly went on, slightly expanding on Andy's actual words. 'And remember, his mum did say he'd been throwing up at the weekend, right?'

For the first time, Tansy looked uncertain. 'True.' She nodded. 'But I still don't get it. Why wouldn't he have the sense to know that if his phone was lost, Melanie's house was the first place to look?'

'I thought of that,' Holly said. 'He says he rang their house, but no one had found it.'

'Oh, very likely,' stormed Tansy.

'And he says that he doesn't want to go near Melanie because she keeps phoning him at home, and popping slushy notes through the door and e-mailing him night and day.'

'And what about not asking me out at all? What's his excuse for that one?' Tansy demanded.

Holly shrugged. 'I don't know, I said you were dead upset.'

'That's right, give him the satisfaction of knowing he's hurt me . . .'

'I did my best!' Holly snapped. 'I thought you'd be pleased.'

'Sorry.' Tansy touched her arm. 'It's just that, well, I know what I want to believe, but I can't take the risk, not till I see him face to face. And I guess that's not going to happen.'

'Oh, yes it is,' Holly beamed. 'Come on, it's time to get your face on. Crunch time is just an hour away.'

6.05 p.m.

'Right, girls, William is in bed, Mrs Morton is downstairs and you've got till nine-thirty . . .'

'Mum, you said ten o'clock,' Holly cut in.

'Argue and you won't be going out at all,' her mother warned. 'Mrs Morton's worried it might snow again.'

'OK.' Holly sighed.

'And if the hospital ring the house, you phone my mobile at once, you understand?' her mother ordered. 'I'll keep it on vibrate just in case.'

'Don't worry,' Holly assured her. 'You look really nice, Mum. You should dress up more often.'

'Angela, will you hurry up?' Holly's dad called impatiently. 'We're running late as it is.'

'Coming,' his wife called back. 'We won't be back till about one in the morning, but I want you two girls in bed . . .'

'Mum? Stop fussing. Go. Like now. Please?'

6.55 p.m.

'I really don't like you going out in this weather,' Cleo's mum protested as Cleo wound a scarf round her neck and scrabbled for her gloves in the hall stand. 'Surely seeing Holly can wait till tomorrow?'

It could, thought Cleo, if it was Holly I was going to see. 'Got to help her with some school work,' she said sweetly. 'She's in an awful muddle. I won't be long honestly.'

Her mum glanced at her watch. 'Roy's late. I do hope this snow isn't holding up his journey.'

I have a horrible feeling, thought Cleo, her stomach lurching, that if anything's preventing him from coming home, it's not the weather.

7.30 p.m. (8.30 p.m. in France)

'How would you like to be, down by the Seine with me / Oh what I'd give for a moment or two, under the bridges of Paris with you . . .'

'Gran!' giggled Jade as her grandmother hit a high note. 'Stop it – people are looking at you.'

'Let them look,' said her grandmother, grinning and hooking her arm through Jade's as they attempted to cross the Champs Elysées. 'If you can't sing when you're in the most romantic city in the world, when can you? Your grandfather and I came here the year before your dad was born and then we brought him here for his thirteenth birthday.'

'Doesn't that make you sad?' Jade gasped. 'I mean, what with Grandpa being dead, and dad gone too, I would have thought it was the one place in the world you would want to avoid.'

Her gran smiled and shook her head. 'It's a funny thing, Jade,' she replied, 'I couldn't have come on my own – but being here with you makes it so right. It's like I'm sharing a special place with the next generation – you!'

Jade felt her eyes prick. 'That's a lovely thing to say,' she said softly.

'So,' her gran replied briskly, shivering slightly as a chill wind gusted round the corner, 'what would the next generation like to do this evening? I thought perhaps a look at the lights from the top of the Eiffel Tower and then –' She paused as Jade's phone rang loudly.

'Hello? Oh, Flynn. Yes, I'm fine – having the coolest time. Sorry, I can't hear properly – the traffic . . .' She stuck a finger in one ear. 'Yes, of course. Call any time you like – tonight about ten would be good. OK, then. *Au revoir!*' She stuffed her phone back in her bag.

'That was Flynn,' she said to her grandmother. 'Why are you looking at me like that?'

Her gran smiled. 'For someone you just met casually on a train,' she said, laughing, 'he certainly knows how to make you look all soppy. Nice boy, is he?'

'He's OK.' Jade shrugged. 'Well, very OK really. But I'm not . . .'

'No, darling, you made that quite clear,' her gran replied. 'You're not into boys. I quite understand.'

8.10 p.m.
Funkie Junkie's – ready to rip!

'I knew it!' said Holly. 'There she is – tarty little madam!' She gestured across the smoky, low-lit music bar. Melanie was sitting in a corner, legs crossed provocatively and her boobs bursting out of a see-through top.

'I'd like to get my hands round her throat,' Tansy began.

'Stop it,' Holly ordered. 'Just keep calm and remember what we planned, OK? Follow me.' She pushed her way across the room. 'Hi, Mel – what are you doing here?'

Melanie's eyes widened. 'What are you doing here? I thought . . .'

'What exactly did you think?' Holly cut in. 'That we'd be the last people you'd see here tonight?'

'I – um, I just meant I didn't think this was your kind

of scene,' Melanie replied. You had to give her credit, Holly thought. She was a quick thinker.

'You meant,' Tansy blurted out, 'that you thought your nasty little scheme would work, right? Sending messages to say tonight was off? Well, you were wrong.'

'I don't know what you're on about,' Melanie said, but even in the dim light, Holly could see the colour spread across her cheeks.

'I'm just here to meet someone,' Melanie went on, looking anxiously across to the doorway.

'Andy, perhaps?'

Melanie's chin jutted out defiantly. 'Yes, actually,' she sneered. 'Not that it's any of your business.'

'Oh, really?' Holly scoffed. 'I have a feeling Andy might not – oh, listen! Isn't that your phone?'

'No!' Melanie snapped.

'I can distinctly hear a phone ringing, can't you, Tansy?' Holly insisted. Good on you, Cleo, she thought. Perfect timing.

'It's not mine, not with that ring tone,' Tansy replied, deliberately taking her phone from the back pocket of her jeans and glancing at it.

'Or mine,' Holly added, moving closer to Melanie and slipping her hand in the pocket of her jacket hanging over the back of the chair. 'Look – it is yours.'

She stared at it. 'Hey, this looks familiar!' She chucked the phone at Tansy. 'I recognise that QPR football sticker, don't you?'

Melanie lunged for the phone.

'You stole Andy's phone,' Tansy began, holding it high above her head out of Melanie's reach.

'And sent foul messages to Tansy,' Holly added

'And lied through your teeth about Andy and you,' Tansy concluded.

'Well, that's where you're wrong,' Melanie snapped back, jumping to her feet and trying to push past Tansy. 'Because Andy wants me, not you. He told me so.'

'Oh, really?' Holly queried.

'Yes, really,' spat Melanie. 'He said he was bored and he wanted someone hot for a change. And I'll tell you one thing, Tansy Meadows . . .' She tossed her head and ran her tongue along her bottom lip. 'He says I'm a much better kisser than you.'

'Oh, did he?' Holly cut in, terrified that Tansy was about to burst into tears. 'Well, perhaps he can tell you again in front of us. He's just arrived. Now we can find out what the real truth is, can't we?'

8.15 p.m.
At last!

'What's with making a phone call and then not saying a word?' Angus queried as Cleo dumped her phone on the table.

'Tactics,' Cleo said with a grin. 'The thing is, my mate Tansy was dumped by her boyfriend but she wasn't really because this girl Melanie had nicked his phone and sent messages to her and tonight we've got this plan going to . . .'

'Cleo,' Angus said, staring at her and swallowing hard. 'Could I kiss you?'

8.16 p.m.
Confrontation

'I think that's my phone, if you don't mind.' Andy held his hand out to Melanie. 'When I phoned, you said you couldn't find it anywhere.'

'It was true,' Melanie stammered defiantly. 'I only discovered it this morning.'

'Liar!' Tansy burst out. 'How come I got messages from it yesterday and the day before?'

'You thought you'd use it to spread lies about me, right?' Andy snapped back, raising his voice above the beat of the sound system.

'I was only telling her –' she jabbed a finger at Tansy '– what you said about dumping her because you wanted me.'

'Andy . . .' Tansy stammered.

Melanie sidled closer to him. 'You don't have to pretend, Andy,' she simpered. 'After what happened on Saturday, there's no going back, is there?' She rested her head on his shoulder and fiddled with a strand of his hair.

'Nothing happened on Saturday,' Andy muttered, shrugging her off, but Holly noticed that he didn't sound as confident as she would have liked.

'Oh, really?' Melanie's tone changed to one of scorn. 'So you never kissed me? Never groped me? Never said I was a million times more fun than that tame old Tansy?'

'Well, thank you, Andy Richards!' Tansy exploded.

'I didn't say that – I wouldn't . . . I don't remember anything!' Andy sounded desperate. 'All I know is I had a couple of drinks, felt dreadful, sat down, thought I was going to throw up . . . and that's all.'

'I've heard it all now,' Tansy burst out again. 'Of all the lame excuses . . .!'

'Dead right,' Melanie agreed. 'Who was it who said "Let's go upstairs, Mel"?'

'I didn't, I wouldn't, I couldn't have,' Andy stammered.

'Really?' Melanie sounded more in charge by the moment, which worried Holly a lot. 'Well, let's see what Tansy makes of this, then!'

She grabbed her own bright pink mobile from her bag, zapped a few buttons and thrust it at Tansy.

'No!' With a strangled cry, Tansy threw it at Andy. 'How could you?'

Holly snatched the phone out of Andy's hand and stared at it. It was the one thing she had prayed they wouldn't find. Proof. It was a picture Andy and Melanie on a white-leather sofa. Snogging. Big time.

'And to think that I believed you!' Holly spat at him. 'How could you?' She grabbed Tansy's hand and turned to go.

'Wait!' Andy shouted. 'It's not what you think, honestly.'

'Oh shut up and go boil your head!' shouted Tansy. And burst into tears.

8.25 p.m.

'I won't cry, I said goodbye, when I changed direction / Past is gone, future's cool, so don't come back to haunt me / Go away, nothing to say, my life's sussed and sor-or-ted / Since I changed / Di-eye-rection!'

Cleo flung her arms upwards as Angus executed a final drum roll. She knew she'd sung better than ever but then when you're in love, she thought, everything was easy.

'Brilliant!' Angus cried, jumping up and hugging her. 'You were great. Are great.' He gave her another nervous kiss, first on the tip of her nose, then her chin, and then finally on her lips. She was about to pull him closer towards her when the door burst open.

'Oh, sorry!' Angus's mother stood in the doorway, smiling broadly, as Cleo jumped backwards and began picking non-existent bits of fluff from her sleeve. 'Don't let me stop you . . .'

'Mum!'

'It's OK, Mrs Walker,' Cleo gabbled. 'I've got to go – my mum will be wondering where I am.'

'Oh, don't go on my account,' Mrs Walker begged. 'Do stay a little longer – Angus would like that, wouldn't you, dear?'

Cleo wondered how the guy managed to live with a woman who treated him like a backward eight-year-old. 'No, really,' she insisted, knowing full well that the moment had been broken. 'See you, Angus.'

'I'll call you,' he assured her, walking with her to the door. 'We'll need to rehearse with the others.' He looked over his shoulder to where his mother stood in the kitchen doorway, still beaming at them both. 'Bye.' He kissed her briefly on the lips and ran a finger over her cheek. 'You're – well, you're lovely.'

8.30 p.m.
Recriminations

'I've just made things worse, haven't I?' Holly said in the taxi on the way home. 'I really believed him when he said that all he'd done was dance with her. Hey, isn't that your phone bleeping?' She shoved a tissue into Tansy's hand and nudged her arm.

'I'm not answering it, not if it's him,' Tansy mumbled, glancing at the phone. 'Oh. It's a text. From Cleo.'

'ANGUS KISSED ME!' she read out loud. '2 X. I AM IN HEAVEN. HOW DID IT GO 2NITE? CLEO XX.'

'Seems everyone else is getting their life together except me.'

'And me,' said Holly. 'Oh, look, the street lights are off – not another power cut, surely?'

'They've been on and off like crazy all evening,' commented the taxi driver. 'Which house, love?'

'The Cedars – just past the next lamppost,' Holly called back.

'I shouldn't worry,' Tansy cut in, as the taxi slowed to a halt. 'If Angus kissed Cleo, he's not gay and if he's not gay, then Kyle must be free . . .'

'Free but not necessarily straight,' Holly reasoned, clambering out of the cab and handing a five-pound note to the driver.

'Well, if you ask me – oh my God!' Tansy grabbed Holly's arm and pointed towards the roof of The Cedars.

Holly froze. Smoke was billowing through a slightly open window and behind, in horror, she saw an orange glow.

'Fire! It's on fire!' she screamed, panic gripping her in the chest like a vice as her stomach heaved. 'Oh my God – Tansy, do something. Call the fire brigade!' She turned to the retreating cab.

'Wait – please, wait!' she yelled, but the driver just kept on driving. The snow covered street was deserted, people's curtains drawn against the cold night. Holly felt she was in a horror movie on freeze frame.

'Where are your mum and dad?' Tansy gabbled, her hands shaking as she punched 999 into the phone

'They're out and . . . oh no! William! William's in there with the babysitter.' She stared at Tansy in wide-eyed horror. 'Come on! We've got to get him out.'

'Hello? Fire – it's an emergency,' Tansy gabbled into the phone as Holly flew up the front drive and rammed her key into the front-door lock with shaking hands.

'Mrs Morton! Mrs Morton!' Holly burst into the sitting room. Mrs Morton, feet up on the coffee table, was snoring softly, a magazine open on her lap.

'Wake up, wake up!' Holly shrieked. 'Tansy, deal with her, I've got to get William.'

'Holly, no!' Tansy tried to grab her arm. 'You'll get hurt. Wait for the fire brigade.'

'There's no time, stupid!' Holly pushed past her and ran up the stairs two at a time. As she turned on to the landing she stopped and gasped. Flames were licking along the carpet, thick black smoke swirling in great clouds towards her. To her horror, she saw that the loft ladder was ablaze and the smoke was billowing through the half-open door of her bedroom, where William would be sleeping on his rollaway bed.

'Holly!' She could hear Tansy's screams behind her. 'Come back!'

Holly hesitated, her mind freezing with fear. She couldn't do it. She couldn't go any nearer. Already her eyes were watering and her nostrils were filled with the acrid smell of smoke. The heat, even at this distance, was scarily intense. She took two steps back, her heart pounding so hard that she felt sure her ribcage would burst open. And then she heard a whimper.

'Mum-mee! Mummy!'

William! *Think, Holly,* she told herself. Wet towels. She ran back to the bathroom, grabbed two towels from the rail and turned on the taps, soaking them as much as she could. And then, clamping one over her nose and mouth and throwing the other over her shoulders, she ran towards the bedroom.

Two minutes later . . . Terrified

Help me, God. Please help me. In a split second of pure horror, she saw flames licking across her carpet; smelled the nauseous odour of melting plastic. Her eyes began stinging so badly she could hardly keep them open as she groped her way through billowing blackness towards William's bed, led only by the sounds of his terrified screams and fits of coughing.

'It's all right, darling,' she began, but a violent paroxysm of coughing rasped at her chest and throat and prevented her from saying any more. The heat was unbearable, even though the flames were at least a metre away from her. She grabbed the little boy and threw the towel from her shoulders over his head, holding it down as firmly as she could as he tried frantically to fight it off.

Get down, a voice said in her head. Safer on the floor. A vague memory of a visit by firemen to her old primary school flashed through her mind and she dropped on to all fours, gripping William. The towel covering her mouth dropped to the floor and she knew she had only seconds to get out. But the door – where was the door? Suddenly the acrid smoke seemed thicker than ever and for a moment she was totally disorientated. Panic gripped her. There was the sound of crashing, splintering wood, and suddenly searing pain shot through her hands.

A flame flared and in that moment she saw the outline of the door. She scrambled on all fours, dragging William with her. It was then she realised he had stopped screaming. His body was limp.

'Please don't let us die,' she prayed, gagging and choking as the pain from burning eyes made her want to vomit. 'Please save us.'

She crawled towards the door. There was a gap between the flames which were starting to lick up the side of the door. She held her breath, stood up, ran and then crumpled to her knees on the landing. It was hot. So very hot. And her chest was tight and her arms felt as if someone had tied weights to her wrists.

The stairs. She had to get to the stairs. She tried to force her eyes to stay open, but the pain was so bad they kept closing despite her efforts. She tried to move but nothing happened. Her head seemed to be growing every second till it felt three times its normal size.

And then she heard feet thundering up the stairs. A

fireman loomed out of the smoke. Holly couldn't speak. She just thrust William at the man. She felt a jet of cold water whoosh past her. And then everything went black.

9.32 p.m.
Frustrated with friends

'Sugar!' Cleo chucked her phone on to the bed in annoyance. No reply from Holly's phone and now no reply from Tansy's either. That was so typical, she thought; I mastermind a great idea and then they don't even bother to let me know how it goes.

She could guess what had happened; they'd sorted it all and were partying away without bothering to text her. Of course, there was another explanation – maybe they were dead jealous about her new relationship, what with Holly being guy-less and Tansy feeling rejected.

WHERE R U? she texted to both phones. CALL ME ASAP OR ELSE. CLEO.

9.35 p.m.
Shock and horror

'Please help her, please,' Tansy sobbed, as a paramedic checked Holly's airway and then clamped an oxygen mask over her soot-blackened face. 'Is she going to die?'

'No way.' The paramedic smiled. 'She was one wised-up kid, getting down to floor level. She's suffering from smoke inhalation right now, and she's got a nasty burn on her left hand and one on the back of her leg, but don't worry, your sister will be fine.'

'She's not my sister, we're just friends,' Tansy told him. 'We've been out in town.'

She looked up at the burning house, its gutted top-floor windows brought into sharp relief by the torches from the fire engine. A police car, sirens blaring, screeched to a halt, skidding slightly on the freezing slush.

'What's – what's going to happen?' she stammered.

The paramedic eyed her as she began shaking uncontrollably. 'Well, we're taking your friend and the little lad to the hospital, and it might be a good idea if you came along too. Shock's a nasty thing.'

'It's all my fault,' Mrs Morton wailed, the blue flashing lights from the police car lighting up her pale face. 'I should never have agreed to babysit what with being so tired and all. I didn't mean to drop off.' She broke down, burying her face in her blue-veined hands.

'Now, don't you worry, my dear,' the paramedic said. 'The kids are safe and that's the main thing.'

'William? Where's William?' Holly's eyelids fluttered and she began coughing, retching and spewing the remains of her supper over the pavement.

'He's safe, thanks to you,' the paramedic said, gesturing to his colleague, who was cradling William in his arms and giving him oxygen. 'But we need to get you two to hospital and contact your mum and dad – do you know where they are?' He handed Holly a wet wipe to wipe her mouth.

'They're at a dinner,' Tansy blurted out. 'I think Holly said it was at the Hilton Hotel.' She looked at Holly, but her friend's head had lolled to one side, her eyes closed once more.

'We'll get someone over there right away,' the paramedic said. 'Let's get you all into the ambulance.'

At that moment, William opened his eyes. 'Fire engine,' he remarked with interest. 'Der-der, der-der.' And then he threw up over the paramedic's feet.

10.10 p.m. (11.10 p.m. in France)
Jade's bedroom. Hôtel de l'Opera, Paris

'Flynn? Hi, how are you?' Jade clutched the phone and leaned back on her pillows. 'Me? I'm having the best time – and guess what? Tomorrow we're going to Montmartre and my gran's going to get one of the street artists to do my picture. Sorry, what did you say?' She was pretty certain she'd heard him right, but she had to make sure. 'See me again? Well, yes – that'd be . . . nice.'

She felt the hugest grin spread across her face. Not that she fancied him or anything – he was just the kind of guy who'd make a really cool mate. 'Sure,' she said. 'I'll call you as soon as I'm back in England. So what have you been doing?'

Suddenly it seemed very important to keep him on the phone for as long as possible.

10.20 p.m.
A&E, Dunchester General Hospital

'Don't go!' Holly rasped, as her friend pulled back the cubicle curtain. 'I'm scared.'

'I'll only be a second,' Tansy assured her, not wanting to admit that the hospital smell was adding to her nausea.

'I'm dying for the loo. Hey, don't cry – it's OK. I'll stay. I'll just cross my legs.'

Holly tried to smile but instead found herself sobbing and coughing. 'Where's William?' she hiccuped, the drip in her arm jerking as she tossed and turned. 'If anything's happened to him . . .'

'He's doing OK,' Tansy reassured her. 'He's had a chest X-ray and they've taken him up to the children's ward. I went to see him while they were doing all those tests on you, and he was asking for chocolate.'

'Thank God.' Holly paused, her body arching with the force of another fit of coughing. 'It was my fault, I know it was. I can't remember snuffing out the tea lights in my bedroom.'

'Don't worry about that now,' Tansy said, sitting on her hands in an attempt to stop their continuous shaking. 'You and Wills are safe, that's all that matters.'

'Holly darling, I'm here!' The cubicle curtain was pulled back and Holly's mum burst in, almost tripping over her long evening skirt. 'Oh, darling!' She perched on the end of the bed and wrapped her arms round Holly, tears pouring down her face.

'I'll just go to the loo,' Tansy murmured. Neither of them replied.

'How bad is it?' Holly gasped in between paroxysms of coughing. 'The house?'

Her mum shook her head, wiping tears away with the back of her hand. 'I don't know,' she admitted. 'I came straight here and Dad went to the house. But it doesn't matter – you and William are OK, that's the important thing. I am so proud of you.' She touched

Holly's bandaged hand gingerly. 'And your poor hand – does it hurt a lot?'

Holly nodded, tears streaming down her face. 'My throat is the worst – it feels as if someone's been up and down it with a garden rake soaked in acid. And I keep being sick.'

Holly bit her lip and took a deep breath. 'I think it was all my fault,' she confessed, 'those tea lights –' she paused for another fit of coughing, gripping the bed frame as her body was racked with the spasms '– I'm not sure whether I snuffed them out.'

'Oh, I'm sure you did,' her mother replied, but Holly saw the brief look of horror cross her face. She'd never forgive herself. Never.

11.00 p.m.

'I'm so, so sorry!' Tansy's mum was breathless as she enveloped Tansy in a hug and looked over apologetically at Holly's mum. 'I got here the instant I heard. Oh my dear, what can I say?' She squeezed Angela's arm. 'And Holly? How's Holly?'

'Alive, thanks be to God.' Tansy saw that Mrs Vine's eyes were full of tears. 'She's got a couple of nasty burns – second degree, they call them – and she's suffering quite badly from smoke inhalation but they say she'll be fine in a day or so.' She flopped down on to a chair.

'They've taken her up to the ward,' she went on, 'and I've got to get back – poor Rupert's having to deal with the mess, and we're both worried sick about the baby and . . .'

'Baby? You don't mean William's hurt?'

'No, it's Serena. She's pregnant again and she's bleeding.'

Clarity said nothing. She just gave Angela a hug. 'I'll pray,' she whispered. 'And by the way,' she continued more briskly, 'tonight you're both coming to my place to sleep. Tansy and I can double up in her room, and you can have mine.' She fumbled in her handbag. 'Here's my spare key,' she said. 'Come whenever you like. Promise?'

Holly's mum gave her a watery smile. 'Thanks,' she replied. 'But I'll have to see what Rupert says.'

'In my experience,' Tansy's mum said smiling, 'when dealing with men, it's best simply to tell them what they're doing.'

Meanwhile . . .

'I'm sorry you have to be on the children's ward, but officially you're still a child,' the staff nurse joked, hooking a chart over the end of Holly's bed and checking the fluid bag on her drip. 'Still, William will be pleased when he wakes up and finds you here.' She pulled the curtains round Holly's bed. 'Now try to get some sleep,' she advised. 'I'll be back every so often to check on you. If you need any more painkillers, just press the bell.'

Holly lay, eyes wide open, staring at the cartoon characters on the curtains. She tried to take her mind off the soreness of her burns and the pain in her chest by thinking about the new baby, but all that filled her mind was the sight of flames, the smell of smoke and the image of William crying in his bed. And it was all her fault. She'd been so eager to get to Funkie Junkie's that she hadn't blown out the candles.

She rubbed her sore eyes with the back of her hand. She knew she stank; even after a thorough wash, helped by the nurse so that she wouldn't get her burns wet, she felt as if she'd fallen into a bonfire. And every time the acrid smell wafted up her nostrils, she felt violently sick.

And then another thought hit her like a thunderbolt. What about all her stuff – her clothes, books, CDs? They were all in her bedroom. What had happened to all that coursework? The stuff she'd sweated blood and tears over for weeks?

She rolled over, buried her face in her pillow and sobbed. She'd moaned like crazy about living in a house that was falling down round her ears. Right now, she would have given anything in the world to have it back again.

Because tonight it felt as if nothing in the world was safe or certain any more.

THURSDAY

The long dark hours of the night . . .

For a lot of people, the night seemed to drag on for ever. Holly tossed and turned in her hospital bed, dozing and then waking up fighting for breath, grabbing at the blankets and retching into a cardboard basin till her sides ached.

Meanwhile, her mother, lying stiff and tense beside her husband in Clarity Meadows' unfamiliar bed, spent the night trying to take on board the fact that, after years of charity work helping homeless and deprived young mums, she was now the one without a roof over her head or the faintest idea of what would happen next.

Holly's dad kept telling himself over and over again that they were so lucky – Holly was safe and little William had escaped unscathed. But try as he would, all he could see in his mind's eye was the last view he'd had of his old family home, its top floor gutted and the windows and doors being boarded up to stop what the police had called 'opportunist looters'. And on top of all that, Naseby, the old cat he'd had for years, was missing. He was glad it was dark in Mrs Meadows' bedroom. That way Angela wouldn't see his tears.

Tansy and her mum tossed and turned for most of the night. Tansy kept thinking she could smell smoke and padded round the house at intervals to make sure they weren't on fire; her mum realised that inflatable beds might look good in the adverts but were far too easy to fall off.

And over in Kestrel Close, oblivious to the fate of her friend, Cleo dreamed that her stepfather and the woman in the lime-green poncho were standing on a revolving stage singing 'Love Is in the Air' and kissing one another in the most revolting, lip-slurping manner. She tried to rush up to them and tear them apart but whenever she got anywhere near they disappeared.

Although she didn't know it, Cleo's stepfather was not enjoying sweet dreams either. He spent a great deal of the night pacing the kitchen floor, drinking countless cups of strong tea and working out just what he was going to say to the family. One thing he knew for sure: he couldn't keep his secret much longer. If he did, he would go mad. Only Jade, stretched out in linen sheets in the stylish hotel off the Rue Madeleine slept with a smile on her face. In her dream, she and Flynn were gliding down a river in a punt and he was feeding her frogs' legs and Roquefort cheese. She didn't like either of them very much, but she ate them. She didn't want to upset him.

8.00 a.m.

'Hello?' Tansy grabbed the phone from the kitchen wall as she slurped her third cup of tea. 'Oh hi, Cleo.'

'Never mind "Oh hi, Cleo,"' snapped her friend. 'Paper round, remember? Mrs Patel's in a right strop.'

'Oh gosh. I forgot. Sorry,' Tansy gasped. 'It's just that what with last night . . .'

'And that's another thing,' Cleo said. 'You might have told me what happened.'

'It was awful,' Tansy admitted. 'I've never been so scared in all my life.'

'Scared? Of Melanie Hankinson? Oh please!'

'Not her, stupid,' shouted Tansy, her already frayed nerves jangling even more. 'She's a slag and a cow.'

'So you didn't make it up with Andy, then?'

'Oh, who cares about all that now? I'm talking about the fire.'

'Fire? What fire?'

'Oh, gosh, I guess you haven't heard, have you?' Tansy replied apologetically and proceeded to fill her in on everything that had happened.

'That's awful,' Cleo gasped. 'The poor things. Are you OK?'

'I feel like crying all the time,' Tansy said. 'But I'm fine really.'

'So what can we do to help – can we go and see Holly?'

'Her mum and dad went to the hospital really early this morning,' Tansy told her. 'They said they'd phone when I could go but I'm not sure I want to.'

'Why?'

'I – I don't know,' she admitted. 'What if she resents me for not helping her get William out?'

'Knowing Holly, she'll resent you a whole heap more if you don't take her the latest *Hot Shots* magazine,' teased Cleo. 'And as it happens, I've got some news that will get her up and about in ten seconds flat. Now, are you coming to do this paper round or not?'

'You don't need me now,' Tansy replied. 'The audition's over.'

'I need you till Saturday,' Cleo said firmly. 'Besides,

you need to fill me in on every last detail of what happened. See you in ten minutes.'

Five minutes later . . .

'Tansy, I honestly don't think you should go out,' her mother said emphatically. 'You're not up to it – all this has been a shock for you.'

'I'll be OK,' Tansy told her. 'It's worse just sitting around thinking. And I'll be with Cleo.' She didn't want to admit that there was also just an outside chance that she might see Andy. Not that she wanted to. Much.

'Well, if you're sure,' her mother said, relenting. 'I'm going to make a few phone calls – let everyone know what's happened and see if we can set up a working party to help the Vines sort out their house. Not that they'll let us in today, I guess. The place will be crawling with fire officers trying to find out what caused the blaze.' She tossed Tansy's mobile phone at her. 'Keep in touch,' she urged. 'Somehow I think today I might be feeling like a rather neurotic mother.'

8.10 a.m.

'There we are, William,' the staff nurse said, plonking William down on the chair beside Holly's bed. 'There's your Auntie Holly.'

Holly turned and gazed at William. His mop of unruly hair had clearly been shampooed and was circling his face like a fuzzy little halo. He grinned at Holly. 'Holly get up now,' he instructed, his voice sounding hoarse and scratchy. 'Play game.'

Holly opened her mouth to tell him she was too tired but no words came out. Instead, she just shook her head and a couple of tears rolled down her cheeks.

'No cry,' ordered William, tugging at the sleeve of her hideous blue hospital gown. 'Play!'

'Later,' Holly whispered, feeling as if it was taking every ounce of energy in her body to form one word. She closed her eyes and ignored William's screaming protests. All she wanted was for the whole world to disappear and leave her alone.

8.35 a.m.

'Are you mad at me about something?' Tansy asked Cleo as they trudged in near silence back to the paper shop. 'You've hardly said a word.'

'It's not you,' Cleo assured her.

'So is it Angus?' suggested Tansy. 'Didn't you say he'd actually kissed you?'

Cleo nodded. 'Mmm,' she murmured.

'Well, don't sound so thrilled about it,' Tansy teased. 'I thought that's what you wanted all along.'

'I did, I do – it's just – can you keep a secret?'

'Of cours.' Tansy nodded. 'What is it?'

'I feel awful worrying about this when Holly's in such a state,' Cleo confessed, 'but it's my stepdad. I think he's having an affair.'

'Oh my God!' Tansy gasped. 'Well, if you think that, then I reckon you've got to get in there and have it out with him. You owe it to your mum.'

8.55 a.m.
In the hotel dining room

'You're very quiet this morning, Jade,' her grandmother observed, plastering her croissant with apricot conserve. 'Thinking about Mum and Dad, are you?'

Jade nodded. 'Two years ago this morning, it seemed like just any other day,' she said with a sigh. 'And by bedtime . . .' She blinked hard and gulped a mouthful of hot chocolate.

'That's why we all have to try to live every moment of our lives to the full.' Her grandmother nodded. 'At least they had a ball while they were alive – all those clubs they belonged to and the theatre trips and things.'

'Gran, can I ask you something?' Jade blurted out. 'Do you think there's something wrong with me?'

'Darling, what an extraordinary thing to say!' her gran exclaimed. 'You're as normal as the next person. Now, what's all this about?'

'Boys,' admitted Jade. 'I can't do them.'

Her gran burst out laughing, and croissant crumbs flew across the tablecloth. 'You make them sound like a rather difficult GCSE subject,' she chortled. 'What on earth do you mean?'

'I go out with a boy, right?' Jade babbled on, determined to get it out now she had started. 'And that's OK for a bit and then they want to get all heavy. It was just the same with Scott: fine to start with and then – well, you know the kind of thing . . .' She doubted her grandmother had the slightest idea, what with being so old, but she didn't want to spell it out.

'Oh, yes – clammy hands, soggy lips and a lot of heavy breathing?' her gran remarked in a matter of fact manner. 'Don't remind me!'

'You mean, you understand?'

'Darling, I haven't always been in my seventies,' her gran reasoned. 'And I'll tell you one thing: boys are boys, whether it's the 1940s or now!'

'But all my friends think snogging is the best thing ever,' Jade said. 'Which must mean I'm abnormal or frigid or something. And I don't know what to do about it.'

'Nothing,' declared her grandmother. 'Do absolutely nothing except be yourself. For heaven's sake, you're only fifteen!' She bit into her croissant and wiped her mouth on a napkin. 'Tell me this,' she went on. 'This lad Flynn you met on the train – what did you like about being with him? And don't say nothing, because I've seen your face every time he texts you!'

Jade shrugged. 'Just the fact that I didn't have to work at being oh-so-trendy, oh-so-sexy Jade,' she admitted. 'I mean, we just chatted about all sorts of stuff and yes, he's a really nice guy.' She bit her lip. 'I guess that with him being in a wheelchair, it was just like chatting to a mate, really.'

Her grandmother smiled.

'What?' Jade asked. 'What are you thinking?'

'Just that I find it hysterically funny that you assume a wheelchair stops a boy from fancying a girl. Another croissant, darling?'

Meanwhile, outside The Cedars . . .

'I can't believe it.' Tansy and Cleo stood stock still, staring at Holly's house. It had been Tansy's idea to walk home the long way round and find out just how bad things were. Now she wished they hadn't bothered. The brickwork on the right-hand side of the top floor was blackened, several windows had been smashed to make way for the fire hoses and the air was heavy with the stench of burnt plastic and melted metal.

'Tansy? Cleo? I thought it was you.' A car pulled up, and Mrs Vine zapped down the window.

'I'm sorry,' Tansy apologised rapidly. 'We weren't being nosy, it was just that we wanted to see for ourselves.'

'It's all right,' said Holly's mum with a sigh, as she climbed out of the car. She glanced at the house, gripping the car door as if frightened of falling to the ground. 'At least they say the ground floor isn't too badly damaged – it's the bedrooms that are ruined,' she murmured.

'Is there anything we can do?' Cleo asked.

'Yes, actually, there is,' Holly's mum replied. 'Go and visit Holly. I'm worried about her. I mean, she's finally stopped coughing and being sick and she's got a bit of colour.'

'That's good,' Cleo said.

'But she's hardly speaking, she won't eat and she keeps crying. The doctor says it's shock, and they'll keep her in for one more day.' She eyed the house once more. 'Not,' she murmured softly, 'that there's anywhere for her to come home to right now.' She turned away, her shoulders heaving.

'We thought maybe if we could take her a few familiar things, she'd feel better,' Holly's dad cut in briskly, slamming the car door. 'But looking at this mess, it doesn't seem very likely.'

'We could take her some make-up and magazines and stuff,' Tansy suggested.

'And I've got some funky new pyjamas I haven't worn yet,' Cleo said. 'They'd fit Holly.'

Holly's mum smiled. 'That would be lovely. The doctor did say that seeing friends of her own age and having a good old gossip might be just the thing. Would you do that?'

'Oh, yes,' Cleo said with a smile. 'If there's one thing we're very good at, it's gossip. Leave it to us.'

10.20 a.m.
Operation Retrieval gets under way

'The announced Tansy's mum, replacing the telephone on its rest. 'Cleo's mum is shopping, Jade's uncle David is going to drive a van round to the house and help salvage what's left and I'm going to make a couple of casseroles – they'll need to eat wherever they end up.'

'You will make it proper food, won't you?' Tansy asked, wrapping a lipstick and cream eyeshadow in silver paper for Holly. 'None of your seaweed and minced nettle fritters.'

'Tansy! When have I ever served seaweed and . . . well, only that once, and I admit they weren't a great success.'

'Mum,' Tansy said, giving her a hug, 'let's face it – you have many talents but cooking is not one of them. Couldn't you just go to Tesco and buy them a pie?'

'Shop-bought food is full of additives and . . . oh heck! Who's that?' The doorbell clanged in a most persistent manner. 'Darling, see who it is, would you? I've still got some calls to make.'

Tansy bit off a piece of Sellotape with her teeth, stuck down the parcel and ran to the front door.

'I came as soon as I heard – are you sure you're OK?' Andy, looking more dishevelled than ever, made to step over the threshold.

'I'm fine,' she replied, blocking his way. 'Not that you'd care.' She knew she sounded sarcastic, but she couldn't afford to fall apart again.

'I wouldn't be here if I didn't care,' Andy replied. 'Your mum phoned mine about the fire, and I just had to make sure for myself that you were in one piece.'

'Well, I am so you can go now,' Tansy said.

'Don't be like that,' he pleaded. 'If anything had happened to you last night, I'd never have forgiven myself.'

'For what? For cheating on me? Or for getting found out?'

'For letting you run off like that, and not explaining everything when I had the chance,' he stressed. 'Look, I don't expect you to believe anything I say, but if you come over to my place in about an hour, I can give you total, complete proof that what happened had nothing to do with me.'

'Oh, like it was a cloned Andy sitting on that sofa, was it?'

He shook his head. 'Please, Tansy, for the sake of what we had together, give me a chance.'

There was a catch in his voice and Tansy could feel her heart melting, even against her better judgement. 'I can't come over,' she retorted. 'I'm going with Cleo to see Tansy in hospital in an hour or so. Her mum says she's really low.'

Andy nodded slowly. 'Poor thing,' he replied. 'But you'll come afterwards? Please.'

No way, thought Tansy. Absolutely not. I'm not going there. 'Yes, all right,' she said. 'I'll be there about four.'

11.20 a.m.

'Angus, it's Cleo. Listen, you know we were meant to rehearse this afternoon? Well, I can't come to your place now. I'm going to see Holly in hospital.' She frowned as he muttered at her down the phone. 'What do you mean, what's wrong with her?' she repeated. 'The fire – oh, gosh, you don't know, do you? Their house was half gutted last night.' She paused, suddenly realising what she'd said. 'I guess you'd better get your parents to phone the Vines,' she gabbled. 'It's probably nothing. The house is probably just fine. I'll call you later. Bye!'

11.45 a.m.

'Hi, Hollyberry!' Holly opened her eyes to see her brother Richard smiling down at her. 'How you doing, sis?'

Holly swallowed hard. 'I'm so sorry,' she whispered. 'I really am – I didn't mean for this to happen.'

'Holly, you saved Wills's life!' her brother interrupted,

snatching her unbandaged hand. 'If it hadn't been for you, he'd have . . .' The words caught in his throat and he turned away.

'You don't understand,' she whispered, tears filling her eyes. 'I left a candle burning and that's why the fire started.' She forced herself to look at him, and she saw what she'd seen before. That fleeting look of shock, horror, that slight clenching of teeth.

'These things happen,' Richard said. 'No one's blaming you.'

She knew he was trying to be kind, trying to make her feel better. But it was no good. She blamed herself. And she always would.

Fifteen minutes later . . .

'Mum? It's Richard.' Holly's brother stood in the car park, mobile phone clamped to his ear. 'I've just seen Holly and I agree. She's really down. Of course, I guess she feels really bad about starting the fire but . . . what? They did? That's brilliant – well, not brilliant, but you know what I mean.' He glanced at his watch. 'I'm due to pick Wills up in a minute, but I'll dash back to tell Holly the news. It'll make her day.'

Five minutes later . . .

'Hey, what are you doing back here?' Holly asked as Richard plonked himself down beside her bed.

'No need to sound so thrilled to see me.' He grinned. 'I've got news from Mum. The fire officer has just checked the house to find out what caused the fire.'

His sister turned her face away. 'We know what caused it,' she whispered. 'Me.'

'That's where you are so wrong!' her brother exclaimed. 'Apparently, it started in the attic – the fire guy said that the whole house needed rewiring. His exact words were that it was a disaster waiting to happen.'

'You mean . . .?'

'It wasn't your fault, Holly,' Richard stressed. 'If anyone's it was Dad's. He's in an awful state about it. Apparently, he was up in the loft the other day clearing stuff and fell over some wires.'

'That's right.' Holly nodded. 'And he swore!'

'Some things never change,' Richard said with a grin. 'Anyway, they say that when the power came on after that power cut you had, there was a surge on the system, the torn wiring couldn't take it and – whoosh! – it just went up in smoke.'

Holly stared at him. 'You're not making this up – you know, to make me feel better?'

'Cross my heart and hope to die,' Richard smiled, making the old gesture from their childhood. 'Be gentle on Dad, though. Right now, he's on a major guilt trip.'

'I know how he feels,' Holly said.

'I've said you can all come and stay with us, but Mum and Dad want to be in Dunchester – there's so much to do. And what with Serena . . .'

'How is she?' Holly asked.

'The bleeding's eased a bit,' he said. 'All we can do is pray. If she loses this baby as well as the others, I don't know how we'll bear it.'

1.35 p.m.
So that's that, then – or is it?

'The Walkers know about the fire, and the sale is off.' Holly's mum slumped down at Clarity's kitchen table and put her head in her hands.

'How did they react?' Clarity asked.

Holly's mum sighed. 'Sadly, Cleo had already spoken to their son and told him,' she replied. 'They were a bit miffed that we hadn't called sooner but what with Naseby – still can't find him – and Rupert's in a state. Silly, really, but he seems more worried about his ruined pikestaffs and old Naseby than he does about anything else.'

'It's the little things that mean the most,' Clarity replied sagely.

'And he's blaming himself for the wiring being a mess and for not having put the loft ladder away and – everything, really.' She rubbed her red-rimmed eyes. 'Well, one thing's for certain, no one is going to touch The Cedars with a barge pole. The whole thing's a disaster.'

'Come off it,' Clarity butted in. 'This could turn out to be a real blessing.'

'And just how,' retorted Holly's mum, 'do you work that one out?'

'Well, if you ask me it's obvious. I'll make another cup of coffee and then I'll tell you.'

Meanwhile, in Kestrel Close . . .

'I'm going to the doctor,' Roy announced, lumbering downstairs in a rather sad pair of cords and a shapeless beige sweater. 'Is your mother still out?'

Cleo nodded. 'She's shopping for Holly's mum.' She waited for one of Roy's sarcastic remarks about money but he merely sighed.

'Awful thing to happen. Losing your home like that in one night. Makes you think, you know. You have to live life to the full while you can. No one knows what's round the corner.'

Cleo eyed him closely. Was having an affair his idea of living life? Was this some overdue mid-life crisis? 'Roy, I saw you the other day . . .' she began.

'Heavens, is that the time?' he cut in. 'Must dash – Dr Abbott hates to be kept waiting.' With that he grabbed his coat and rushed out of the door. I'll have him, Cleo thought determinedly. Tonight, come hell or high water, I'll have him.

And back at Tansy's house . . .

'You know, you could be right,' said Holly's mum, sipping her coffee and eyeing her friend admiringly. 'And if you are . . .'

'Your worries are over,' Clarity said, laughing. 'See what Rupert thinks and then go for it. You've nothing to lose.'

2.35 p.m.

'Go on, put the lipstick on,' Tansy urged after she had helped Holly open her parcel. 'See if it suits you.' She caught sight of Holly's bandaged hand. 'Hey, let me do it for you,' she suggested.

'Later.' Holly smiled wanly. 'But thanks a lot. It's

really kind of you.' There was a flatness about her voice that worried Tansy.

'Have a chocolate,' Cleo suggested, passing Holly the box of Quality Street she'd bought her.

'You go ahead,' Holly replied, chewing her bottom lip. 'I'm not really hungry.'

'OK, that's enough,' Tansy insisted. 'What's wrong?' She paused. 'Sorry. Dumb thing to say,' she muttered. 'Are you in pain? Is it the burns?'

Holly shook her head. 'It's just – it's just . . .' She burst into tears. 'Now look what you've done,' she accused them. 'You've made me blub.'

'So?' Cleo smiled. 'What's a blub among mates?' She put an arm round Holly's shoulder. 'Can we do anything?'

'Like redo all my coursework? Like start a model for art and design all over again? Like rebuild my house?' The tears were falling fast now and Cleo rummaged in her bag for a scrunched-up tissue and shoved it into Holly's hands. 'Loads of my school stuff was in my bedroom,' Holly sobbed. 'It'd be all right for you two, because you're brain boxes, but it took me for ever and the art was the one thing that was going right, well, that and the English, but the English is OK, I guess, because it's not so hard.'

'Stop right there!' Tansy ordered, cutting in on her incoherent gabble. 'Do you really think anyone on the planet cares about all that? You're alive, that's what matters.'

'And we can all pitch in and help you sort out the coursework,' Cleo added.

'Thanks.' Holly tried to smile. 'That's really kind and – oh my God! Look who's just rolled up.' Cleo and Tansy turned.

Andy was striding across the ward. And the expression on his face was one of grim determination.

Meanwhile, in the artists' quarter of Montmartre . . .

'*C'est tres jolie, n'est-ce pas?*' The pavement artist, looking like a cliché of the Frenchman in his striped shirt and ill-fitting beret, handed Jade her portrait. '*C'est un cadeau pour votre mère, non?*' Jade swallowed hard and shook her head. 'Ah!' the man cried, a broad grin on his face. 'For ze boyfriend, yes? He will think you are so beautiful!' With the compliment came a hand outstretched for payment.

'There we are,' Jade's gran declared, placing a pile of Euros into his hand and hooking her arm through Jade's. 'Now I think it's time for those cakes we've been promising ourselves.'

'Sorry, Gran,' sniffed Jade, brushing a tear from her eye. 'It's just that when people talk about Mum or Dad when I'm not expecting it, I get all upset.'

'I know, darling. It happens to me all the time,' her grandmother confessed. 'And frankly, it doesn't matter. If people can't handle a bit of grief, then that's their problem. Hey, do you remember how your Dad loved cream horns?'

Jade giggled. 'And remember the day Mum tried to make them and they collapsed when she took them out the oven and Dad said it didn't matter, he'd have cream with no horn?'

'So let's go find some cream cakes and have them in their memory – what do you say?'

Jade was relieved to see that her Gran was struggling not to cry too. Somehow it helped to know she wasn't the only one whose heart still hurt a lot. *'Bien sûr!'* She smiled. 'Lead the way, *grand-mère!'*

They were crossing a cobbled street and eyeing up the window of the nearest patisserie when Jade's phone rang. 'It's Paula!' she gasped. 'Hi, Paula – yes, we're having a brilliant time thanks. Are you OK? What?' Her mouth dropped open as she listened to her aunt's words. 'Oh my God, a fire? Was anyone hurt?' She caught sight of her grandmother's startled expression. 'Not our house, Holly's,' she mouthed. 'Sorry, Paula – what did you say? In hospital? But she's going to be OK?' She closed her eyes. 'Yes of course I will. Don't be silly, I'm glad you told me. If you see her mum tell her to give Holly my love, OK.'

She flipped the phone off and stared at her grandmother. 'What is it about February 20th?' she asked with a choke in her voice. 'Will it always be a bad news day?'

Meanwhile, back in Paddington Ward . . .

'Hi, Holly, how are you doing?' Andy thrust a bar of Toblerone at her.

'I was getting better till I saw you,' she retorted, her voice still croaking and harsh. 'I don't think Tansy wants you here.' And neither do I, she thought miserably. I just want to sleep.

'Well, that's tough, because I'm here,' Andy replied. The three girls eyed one another in astonishment. Andy and assertiveness didn't usually go together. He turned to Tansy. 'I know you said you'd call in later,' he went on, 'but I figured you might bottle out – and anyway, Alex has got circuit training at half-past four so it had to be now.'

'What's Alex got to do with it?' Tansy demanded.

'You'll see.' He marched over to the door of the ward and beckoned. Alex, dressed in a red and white tracksuit and looking decidedly sheepish, shuffled into the room. 'Right,' Andy said. 'Tell her, Alex. Tell it like it really was.'

Alex took a deep breath. 'Last Saturday, Andy came along to Ella's party, right?'

'The party he said he wouldn't go to if it was the last rave on earth – that one?' Tansy cut in sarcastically.

Alex ignored her. 'Ella told me that Melanie really fancied Andy,' he went on, 'and wouldn't it be a laugh if the two of them got off together?'

'So you told her that Andy was with Tansy and totally out of bounds?' Cleo interrupted, holding his gaze.

He looked away. 'I guess I should have said something but . . .'

'But what?' Cleo demanded.

'It was difficult,' he muttered.

'Oh, right!' Cleo went on. 'Like your mouth was suddenly stapled closed, was it? Or you'd forgotten the words "No way, idiot head"?'

Go girl, thought Holly, smiling despite the pain that was shooting through her fingers.

'Ella was – well, she'd been saying I was boring,' Alex

mumbled, his face flushing scarlet. 'I thought she was about to dump me and I wanted to show her I was up for a laugh. But when I saw what she was going to do . . .'

'Which was?' Tansy and Cleo chorused together.

'She got Andy a Pepsi, and she put three shots of vodka into it. He downed it in one.'

'Oh and you let him!' Tansy exploded. 'Some mate.'

'I'm not his bloody mother!' Alex exploded. 'Anyway, didn't think it would have that effect. I mean, it was obvious he'd get a bit tipsy, but I didn't expect him to be totally out of it.'

Tansy eyed Andy closely. 'Three vodkas isn't enough to make you snog that tart,' she said acidly. 'You must have wanted to.'

'I'd already had a couple of beers,' Andy admitted. 'I was so angry with . . . well, after the row with my parents I just lost it. So I had a couple of drinks as soon as I got there to get me in the mood.'

'For what?' muttered Tansy.

'Anyway, me and Ella carried on dancing,' Alex said, 'and then after a bit, we went through to the front room and that's when I saw Andy on the sofa with Melanie and she was kissing him.' Tansy wanted to speak but somehow her throat had closed up. 'Ella thought it was a right laugh, and so when Mel asked her to take a picture, she did,' Alex went on.

'On Melanie's phone,' Holly chipped in.

Alex continued, 'But Tansy, the point is, Andy was totally out of it. Melanie was throwing herself at him and he couldn't have fought her off, the state he was in.'

'Really?' Tansy whispered.

'Really,' Alex insisted. 'I was a jerk to let it get out of hand. Especially since Ella dumped me anyway.'

'Lucky you,' muttered Holly.

'But, please,' Alex begged, 'can't you two just make up? Then I can get out of here – I hate hospitals.'

'You go,' Tansy told him. 'Andy and I have got a bit of talking to do.'

'Talking, or yelling?' Alex asked anxiously.

'Talking,' Tansy said. 'In private.'

'Oh, good,' Alex said with a smile. 'Mission hopefully accomplished.'

In Tansy's house, clearing the air

'And you promise that you didn't fancy Melanie – not even for a minute?' Tansy repeated for the third time.

'I swear it,' Andy said. 'Credit me with a bit of taste. So, please – can we forget all this and start over?' Tansy put her arms round his neck and kissed him. 'I take it,' he said with a smile of relief, 'that means yes?'

Half an hour and three-quarters of a tub of Chunky Monkey ice cream later . . .

'So Cleo's singing at Rock Hard?' confirmed Andy, after Tansy had filled him in on the events of the past few days – edited version.

'Yes, but don't say a word to your parents,' Tansy warned. 'Cleo's lot are dead against her doing stuff with the band and if it gets out she's going to be in dead trouble.'

'The chance of me having more than two words with my parents is pretty remote,' Andy replied grimly.

'So what's going on?'

'I don't know where to start,' he stammered. 'Mum and Dad – they keep arguing. They've always had the odd row, but this is much worse.' He shook his head. 'They were at it again on Saturday night,' he explained. 'That's why I stormed off and went to the party. I just couldn't hack it any more.' He put his head in his hands. 'I'll never forgive myself.' His voice dropped to a whisper and Tansy edged closer. 'If I'd stayed at home and not gone to the dumb party, it would never have happened.'

'What wouldn't have happened?'

'All the hitting and throwing things.'

'Your dad lashed out?' She couldn't believe it – Mr Richards was a complete softie. Andy stared at her, his face turning purple, whether with embarrassment or rage Tansy couldn't tell.

'No,' he replied. 'My mum did. She's done it before. Tansy, I think my mum's going mental.'

Explanations

'So the cut on your dad's face, the one he said he'd got quad biking?' Tansy queried.

'Mum did it.' He was struggling not to cry. Tansy squeezed his hand. 'When I threw up at the party, Ella's mum sent me home in a taxi and rang my mother – when I got home Mum went ballistic.'

'I can imagine.' Tansy nodded.

'Anyway, next morning Dad tried to make a joke of

it – you know, saying that all guys did it at least once and it wasn't that big a deal.'

'That was cool of him,' Tansy murmured, wondering what her mother's reaction would have been under similar circumstances.

'My mum didn't think so,' Andy replied. 'She just turned on him, lashing out, calling him names . . .'

'What did he do?'

'Nothing.' Andy's voice was flat. 'Even when she slammed into his face with her fist and scratched him, he just stood there and took it. He didn't even try to push her away.' Suddenly he thumped the table. 'All he did was put his arms round her afterwards and say it was all OK, and not to worry. And she said she was sorry and it wouldn't happen again and . . .'

'So that's good,' Tansy said. 'but why didn't you answer the phone when I called? We could have talked and . . .'

'Dad was going to phone the doctor – you know, to get Mum some calming-down pills or something – and she yanked the thing from wall and smashed it on the floor. OK, laugh!'

'I'm not laughing,' Tansy assured him. 'Your mum needs help, Andy.'

'Try telling her that,' Andy retorted sarcastically. 'She just says she's fine and it won't happen again and Dad goes along with it. We even got a sitter for the twins and went out to a movie and supper on Monday and played at happy families. Great. Except that on Tuesday it happened again. All because Dad put a pink towel in with the babies' nappies. She screamed and threw stuff and that's when the neighbours called the police.'

'Andy I know it must have been awful,' Tansy said. 'But why shut me out? Why didn't you ask me out with your dad and Ricky?' Even as she asked the question she knew the answer.

'Like it's really something you want the world to know about?' he snapped. 'I wanted to have it out with my dad with no one else around. I'm so angry with him – the way he just keeps forgiving her and letting it happen again and again and not getting any help.' He chewed his bottom lip. 'And then, what with Melanie hassling me every five minutes and Ricky crying all the time and wetting the bed and the babies screaming whenever Mum shouted – I just couldn't cope with making excuses.'

'I understand,' Tansy said, because suddenly she did. She remembered how she felt when she was trying to find her real father – how even telling Andy was just too difficult to think about. 'So are things any better?'

Slowly, Andy nodded and gingerly took Tansy's hand. 'Telling you makes it a bit more bearable,' he admitted. 'Only if you ever breathe a word . . .'

'As if!' Tansy objected. 'But do you think it would be an idea to get my mum to chat to yours? They're good friends, after all, and she's already sussed that something's wrong.'

Andy shrugged. 'What good's that going to do? Mum pretends everything's fine all the time – till it isn't.'

'I don't know,' Tansy admitted, 'but maybe it's got something to do with having the babies?' She faltered, knowing that the one topic Andy wouldn't want to talk about was just who the father of the twins might be. 'I didn't want to tell you this, but you remember a few months back, when your mum lent me that jacket of hers?' Andy nodded. 'Well, we found a keyring with a photo of the twins in and a note.'

Andy frowned. 'A note to who?'

'It just said, "Here's a memento of our beautiful babies. Can't wait to see you."'

Andy's neck was turning a livid shade of red. 'So? I guess it was for my aunt. Or Mum's friend in Paris.'

'But it went on to say, "Wish things were different."' Tansy finished. 'Andy, I'm not probing, I'm not prying, I just think that with everything that's gone on, your mum may need help and support. And my mum is her friend after all.'

'It's all supposed to be a secret,' Andy said miserably. 'If Mum found out you knew anything . . .'

'She won't. I promise.'

'Well, OK,' he agreed. 'We might as well try anything, because I know for sure we can't go on like this.'

4.20 p.m.

'Angus? It's me, Cleo. Look, you know we need to rehearse tomorrow – well, I've got this great idea because –'

'Cleo! Cleeee-oh!' A door slammed and feet thundered up the stairs.

'Hang on,' she muttered down the phone, as her bedroom door flew open and her stepfather, red in the face, burst in. 'Just what the hell do you think this is?'

Cleo's heart missed a beat. Roy was waving a copy of the *Evening Telegraph* above his head, and she knew for certain what he'd seen. 'Got to go, I'll ring you back!' She threw her phone on the bed as Roy stabbed a finger at the paper.

'*Local band head for the big time!*' he shouted, reading out the headline. '"*Schoolgirl Klioh*" – my God, they can't even spell! – "*is local band KickStart's big hope for a place on* WaveBand, *TV-K's answer to* Pop Idol."' He flung the paper on to the floor.

'Where did you get that?' Cleo gasped.

'Doctor's surgery,' he snapped. 'Surprised I didn't spot it last night.' He glowered at her. 'Well? What have you got to say for yourself? Your mother told you quite clearly that singing with this – this load of louts . . .'

'You don't know them – they are not louts!' Cleo cut in.

'The fact remains that you went behind our backs, and the one thing I won't have from anyone in this house is deceit!'

That was when something inside Cleo's brain snapped. 'Oh, really! So how come you tell us you're at meetings when you're not?' Even over her own shouting she heard Roy's sharp intake of breath. 'How come,' she ranted on, 'you say you're in Milton Keynes when all the time you're with some other woman?'

'You're talking rubbish,' he snapped back.

'No, I'm not!' she exploded. 'You want to know where that picture of me and the band was taken? At Dunchester College. On Tuesday.'

Roy's shoulders sagged.

'And I saw you chatting up some woman . . .'

'I was not chatting her up,' Roy cut in. 'It was a business discussion.'

'Pull the other one!' Cleo shouted. 'So on Wednesday in Guildhall Road you had another discussion, did you? Climbing into her car and kissing her? That kind of discussion?'

'Cleo, will you just shut up talking about things you know nothing about?' her stepfather argued. 'We're talking about you, not me. What do you think your mother is going to say when she sees this garbage?' He kicked the newspaper across the floor.

'And what's she going to say when she hears about you and your other woman?' Cleo shouted back, her voice cracking with emotion. 'My dad cheated on her years back, remember? Well, I'm not going to let anyone else do it to her ever again!'

Roy's face softened. 'Cleo, I'm not cheating on anyone, I promise,' he said with a sigh. 'The truth is I met up with Judy to talk about a possible job lecturing at the college.'

'Get real!' Cleo shouted. 'You've got a job.'

Roy stared at her, his jaws working. 'No, Cleo, that's the whole point,' he said, sinking down on the end of her bed. 'I haven't got a job. They've made me redundant.'

Explanations

'I still don't get it,' Cleo said, after Roy had explained about new management, office relocation and at the end, reluctantly, how his face never fitted after a major bust-up with the new MD which included throwing a

148

waste bin across the desk and calling him a Number One Nerd. 'I mean, why didn't you just tell us?'

Roy shook his head. 'I thought, what with the redundancy package and everything, I'd find a new job and then I could make it sound really upbeat for your mum. You know how depressed she's been – I could hardly come clean and make her even worse, could I?' Cleo hoped that the surprise didn't show on her face. She'd never thought of Roy as being someone with compassion. 'That's why I pretended to be going to work each day,' he said. 'Dumb, I know, but somehow . . .' There was a catch in his voice. 'I couldn't admit even to myself that I was a failure.' He looked across at Cleo. 'Well, go on, say it,' he challenged her.

'Say what?' she asked.

'That your real dad has got a good job, that your real dad would never have been such a fool, that your real dad is loads better than me . . .'

'Is that what you think I believe?' she asked. 'Roy, I know you and I don't hit it off all the time, but at least you're here. My dad went off with someone else without a backward glance.' She bit her lip. 'And I reckon you care about Mum – deep down.'

'I do, you know that,' Roy began, as downstairs a door slammed. 'Oh God, it's your mother back with Lettie!' Roy gasped. 'Not a word . . .'

'Hold it right there,' Cleo said. 'You've got to tell her. She's bound to find out . . .'

'Not if you don't tell her,' Roy stressed. 'Oh and by the way – you needn't think any of this makes any difference to what I said. You are not singing with any band and that's final!'

5.00 p.m.

Holly had just given up all attempts at eating what the hospital assured her was a toasted cheese sandwich when Leo Bellinger from the *Evening Telegraph* came striding over to her bed.

'Hi, Holly!' he said with a grin. 'Are you ready for the in depth interview?'

Holly frowned. 'What do you mean?'

'"*Local girl rescues toddler from blazing house*",' quoted Leo, whipping out his notebook and pulling the cap off his pen with his teeth. 'The editor thought that a piece in your own words about what it felt like would make a good follow-up to the photo of the house in today's edition.'

'Our house? There's a picture?' Holly gasped.

'Sure,' he said, pulling a copy of the paper from the inside pocket of his jacket. 'See?'

She stared at the paper. The picture had been taken while the fire engines were still jetting foam and water at the upstairs windows. Billows of smoke stood out against the floodlights, and the photographer had caught a wooden shutter crashing to the ground ablaze. Holly began to shake. As she shook, the feeling of nausea rose in her throat and her teeth began to chatter. And then she began to cry as if her heart would break.

7.30 p.m.
Evening visiting in Paddington Ward

'They say you can come home tomorrow, darling,' Holly's mum told her.

'Home?' Holly whispered. 'We haven't got one.'

Her mother patted her hand. 'Not right now,' she admitted, 'but the hotel will do for a few days, and next week we're going to find a nice house to rent till the insurance is sorted out and we decide what to do.' She winked at Holly. 'And as soon as you're fit enough, you've some shopping to do. How do you feel about a nice wad of money to spend on clothes and CDs?'

'Great!' Holly smiled broadly for the first time. 'Oh, gosh, what shall I wear tomorrow? I can't walk out of here in Cleo's pyjamas.'

'You're in luck,' her mother said. 'There was a whole load of your stuff drying in the laundry room – the fire didn't touch those. There's enough for a couple of days.'

'So can I go shopping tomorrow?' Holly asked. She looked at her bandaged hand. 'Then again, perhaps not.'

8.00 p.m.

Cleo was about to wash her hair when her phone rang.

'Cleo? It's Kyle. We missed you at rehearsal this afternoon. Are you on e-mail?'

'Yes, why?'

'I need to e-mail you the final changes to that last chorus.'

'It's cuteycleo@hotmail.com,' she told him. 'Silly address, I know. I invented it when I was much younger.'

'So how's Holly?' he asked.

'Not too bad,' Cleo said, 'but I reckon she needs cheering up. Hey, I've got a great idea – why don't you go and see her tomorrow?'

'Me? She hardly knows me.'

Go for it, she told herself firmly. Love is the best tonic in the world. 'Look, I'll let you into a secret – she's really keen on you,' she informed him. 'In fact, when Angus and I started getting it together, she was dead excited because . . .'

'You what?'

'Oh it's early days, but you know . . .'

'No I don't know,' Kyle argued. 'What's Angus been saying?'

'That's between him and me,' Cleo replied flirtatiously. 'But if I told you what we all used to think . . .'

'Look, I've got to go,' Kyle cut in. 'Things to deal with.'

'But you'll go and see Holly?' Cleo urged. 'At least think about it?'

'Oh, I'll think about it,' Kyle agreed. 'I can promise you that.'

FRIDAY

8.50 a.m.
3 Plough Cottages. Calling for reinforcements

'I don't see,' Tansy's mother told her, perching on the end of Tansy's bed, 'how I can go barging into Andy's house and demanding that Val tells me all her problems.'

'It's easy,' Tansy told her firmly. 'You can pretend to be asking her to help Holly's mum and dad.'

'I did that. She said life was hectic and she couldn't leave the twins.'

'That proves it,' Tansy insisted. 'She's a really nice person – she'd never refuse normally. Go on, Mum, you know how good you are at sorting people out.' She paused. 'Well, other people anyway. Not so hot on your own life.'

'I love you too,' teased her mother. 'OK, I've got the morning off so I'll give it a go – but don't hold your breath.'

Seconds later . . .

Cleo was making her fourth slice of toast when Roy came into the kitchen.

'Right,' he said briskly. 'While she's out you and I need to talk.'

'Exactly,' she cut in. 'Roy, Mum's just gone out in her dressing gown. She's as miserable as anything, and I'm really worried.'

'So worried that you make things worse by going behind her back?'

'I'm sorry,' she replied. 'Really.' She put a downcast expression on her face and looked at him with what she hoped were big, pleading eyes.

'Anyway, it doesn't matter. It's not like we got through the audition. It's all over for us.'

'You never told me that,' he replied.

'You didn't give me the chance,' she said meekly, while inwardly bristling at the expression of pleasure that crossed her stepfather's face.

'Well, I'm pleased to hear it,' he replied. 'And on this occasion, considering how low your mum is, I won't let on to your mother just how deceitful and underhand you've been.' He paused. 'Provided, that is, that you keep your mouth shut about my job.'

She held his gaze. 'That's blackmail,' she murmured, her brain working overtime. On the one hand, she couldn't let Roy get one over on her. On the other, if her mum found out what she'd done, she would most definitely ground her and then Rock Hard would be a non-starter.

'Your choice,' Roy said, and Cleo heard the note of pleading underlying his false bravado.

'OK,' she said, sighing. 'But if you don't get a job with this Judy, you've got to come clean.'

'Give me till the end of the weekend, OK?' her step-father asked.

Perfect timing, she thought. 'You're on,' she said. 'Good luck.'

10.45 a.m.
On the way to the Gare du Nord

'It's been a brilliant trip, Gran – thank you so much!' Jade squeezed her gran's arm as they sat in the back of the taxi.

'I've loved every moment,' her grandmother replied. 'It's been a real treat.'

'So what shall we do tomorrow?' Jade asked.

'Tomorrow?' her gran said. 'Well, I'll get you to the station for an early train home, I guess.'

'But you said I could stay over till Sunday,' Jade protested. 'We agreed.'

'I know, darling,' her grandmother nodded. 'But surely you want to get back to see Holly – bless her, she'll need all the friends she can find right now.'

'She's got the others,' Jade said. 'And, besides, they'll all be going off to this rock concert which is so not me.'

Her gran frowned. 'I doubt Holly will be going anywhere for a while,' she replied. 'You could spend the evening with her, cheer her up.'

Jade shook her head. 'I'd rather stay with you,' she murmured.

'Funny,' her gran mused. 'I thought Holly was the one person who was there for you when you started at West Green school? The person who understood how you felt after Mum and Dad died, the one who never wandered off if you burst into tears? Obviously I got it wrong.'

Jade nodded slowly. 'You're right,' she said. 'I ought to go back. I'm being selfish.'

Her gran nodded. 'And of course, the sooner you get home, the sooner you can phone this Finn . . .'

'Flynn,' said Jade, savouring the word and smiling to herself.

'Yes, him,' her gran said, nodding. 'The only-a-mate-nothing-serious guy. Him.'

Meanwhile, back at the hospital, being discharged . . .

'How's Serena?' Holly asked her mum as they waited for the nurse to give them Holly's discharge papers.

'The bleeding's stopped,' her mother replied. 'But they're keeping her in for another day just to be on the safe side. She's a bit anaemic and . . .' She broke off as the nurse reappeared.

'Right, that's five days' worth of antibiotic tablets, a pack of dressings, antiseptic cream – and we'll see you at Outpatients next Monday.' The nurse beamed at Holly and her mum. 'And if you get any more coughing or chest pain, you let us know right away, OK?'

Holly nodded. 'I can go out, can't I?' she asked.

'Busy social life, have you?' The nurse laughed.

'I'm going to Rock Hard on Saturday,' Holly said. 'That's a band festival . . .'

'You don't have to tell me,' grinned the nurse. 'My boyfriend's in one of the bands. There's this TV programme they're going to make and there's a contest on to find . . .'

'Let's go, Mum,' Holly cut in rapidly. 'I suddenly feel I need some fresh air. Like now.'

10.50 a.m.
Heart to heart

'Val, sorry to bother you but I need a quick word.' Tansy's mum stepped over the threshold of the Richards' house before Val could stop her. 'About the kids.' She knew that any hint of things being wrong with Andy would get his mother's attention.

'They're OK, aren't they?' Val asked anxiously. 'I know I was a bit tough on Tansy at first, but that's when I thought she'd been at the party and . . .'

'They're fine,' Clarity assured her. 'All lovey-dovey again. It's you I'm worried about.'

'Me? I'm fine,' Val replied defensively. 'Why? What have people been saying?'

'Why don't you put the kettle on, and I'll shove these on a plate?' Clarity waved a bag of Danish pastries in the air. 'Then we can have a good chat.'

11.00 a.m.
Dust and ashes

'Are you sure this is a good idea?' Holly's mum said as her father turned the car into Weston Way. 'Holly's only just out of hospital, after all.'

'I want to see the house, Mum,' Holly interrupted firmly. 'I need to.'

Her father pulled up outside the house, carefully avoiding a large skip at the bottom of the driveway.

The moment she was out of the car, Holly legs turned to water and she began trembling from head to foot. 'Can we go in?' she whispered.

'Only downstairs,' her father told her. 'The fire people are still putting in props to make sure the rest of the ceilings stay up.'

They clambered over charred bits of wood and twisted metal into the hall. The stench of smoke mixed with mildew hit Holly in the face and she wanted to retch.

'My bedroom?' Holly faltered, peering up the stairwell.

Her mother bit her lip. 'It's . . . well, it's pretty much gone, Holly,' she told her, putting an arm round her shoulders. 'The fire started in the loft right above your room – I'm so sorry.'

Holly's face crumpled. 'Is there anything left?' she sobbed. 'What about all my photos and all my old school stuff?' Her mum's silence told her all she needed to know. 'So my model's gone then,' she wept. 'The only thing I was any good at.' She could feel anger welling up inside her.

'That's where you're wrong,' her mum said. 'It's in the boot of my car.'

'What? How?'

'You left it in the kitchen on Tuesday,' her mother replied. 'It was in my way when I was doing the ironing, so I shoved it out into the garage to dry. I rescued it last night.'

Holly gave her a hug. 'Thanks, Mum,' she said. 'I know it seems like a little thing, but it's the best bit of coursework I've ever done. And when you're as useless as I am at everything else . . .'

'Holly Vine, don't you ever say that again!' her father cut in. 'Thanks to you, half the house is still standing, my grandson is safe and well and you are only slightly damaged. Useless? I don't think so.'

For the first time in her life, Holly saw her father cry. Within seconds, her mum had joined in. Somehow, it made things easier. If they could cry, then maybe it was OK for her to have another good howl too.

Five minutes and a lot of tissues later . . .

It was a mess. Even downstairs, where the fire hadn't reached, the carpets were wet and filthy from the trampling of fire officers, the air heavy with the smell of burning and chemicals. Gazing up the stairwell, Holly could see the blackened ceiling and burned banisters and she could only guess at the horrors that lay out of sight.

'I'm going outside, Mum,' she called to her mother who was emptying papers from her bureau in the study.

She walked through the kitchen, averting her eyes from the huge patch of damp on the ceiling, and out the back door. As she ambled down the garden, shivering slightly in the chill wind, a whole flood of memories swamped her – the huge garden she played in as a child, before her father sold the vegetable plot to a builder for new houses; Paul, the guy who had moved in to one of them, and with whom she'd been passionately in love; her fourteenth birthday party and the disaster of the gatecrashers . . .

She jumped out of her skin as something moved against her leg, almost tripping her up. 'Naseby!' She dropped to her knees as the cat mewed and rubbed against her. He was thinner, his usually sleek coat was filthy and his skinny legs trembled. But he was alive. She tried to pick him up, but the bulky bandage on her hand made it difficult, and clearly Naseby was not at all keen on the smell of antiseptic.

'Dad! Mum! Quick!' she shrieked, terrified that he would disappear again. 'Come here!'

'Darling, what is it? Are you OK?' Her father flung open a window and leaned out.

She pointed to the cat and grinned. 'Naseby!' Leaving the window flapping in the wind, he disappeared and in an instant was out of the back door, scooping the cat up in his arms and burying his face in his fur.

'Thank God,' he breathed as the cat began to purr tentatively.

He turned to Holly and smiled. 'There you are, you see. You come home and everything starts coming right again.'

Ten minutes later . . .

'Right, we'll get you back to the hotel, then I'm off to get Naseby checked over at the vet's,' Holly's dad declared, coaxing Naseby into the cat basket he had retrieved from the garage. 'And, Angela, you go to the estate agents and see about renting a house – I don't want Naseby at the cattery for a day more than is necessary.'

'But first we have to stop off and get me a new phone,' Holly said. 'I can't find mine. I think it fell out of my pocket in the fire.'

'Holly, we have to deal with the important stuff first,' her father insisted. 'Trivial things must wait.'

'Dad,' Holly said with a sigh, 'you are seriously sad. What is more important than a mobile phone?'

11.15 a.m.
Andy's house. Three cups of coffee, a box of tissues and two pastries later . . .

'So I guess you won't want anything to do with me now you've heard all that,' Andy's mum said as Clarity cleared away their mugs.

'Don't be silly,' she replied. 'I'm not a fair-weather friend, but you do need help. You know that, don't you?'

Mrs Richards nodded. 'I should never have come back,' she said flatly. 'You know, after I left Allan and the kids.' Clarity said nothing. She knew there was more to come. 'Maybe I should never have had the twins. But I couldn't bear the thought of getting rid of them, even though they weren't Allan's, and he said he'd cope with anything, just to have me back in his life. I've let him down so badly. Why am I so horrid to him? Why do I lose it so often? Am I going mental?'

'I reckon,' Clarity said, 'that you've got post-natal depression.'

'But that starts the moment the baby is born,' Val protested.

'That is so not true,' Tansy's mum assured her. 'It can hit months later. I had a really low patch when Tansy was ten months old. And it can change people, you know – but loads can be done.'

'Like shoving me in a mental hospital and loading me with drugs, you mean?' she retorted. 'No way.'

'Now you're being silly,' Clarity said, picking up the phone.

'What are you doing?'

'Getting you an appointment with the doctor,' said Tansy's mum. 'And I'm coming with you. No one gets put on drugs while I'm around.'

11.50 a.m.
Get me back in touch!

'This is so wicked,' Holly breathed, fingering her brand new, bright purple video phone. 'I wish I didn't have to wait like for ever for them to register my number and get it working.'

'Holly, they said four hours,' said her mother, with a sigh. 'Nothing life-changing is going to happen in that time.'

Holly said nothing. As remarks went that one was pretty dumb. They only had to think back to Wednesday night to realise that.

12.45 p.m.

Cleo was grappling with her history essay when her mobile rang.

'Cleo, it's Kyle. I'm trying to get hold of Holly, but when I dial her number it's just dead.'

'She lost her phone in the fire,' Cleo said. 'She told me at the hospital. Ring her at the hotel – The Grange on Bedford Road. Are you going to see her?'

'I don't know – I thought she might like to come to the rehearsal this afternoon – at Angus's place, though' he said.

'She might not feel up to it,' Cleo reasoned. 'She only got out of hospital this morning.'

'True – OK, I'll call by in a bit. See you at five. And Cleo?'

'Mmm?'

'About you and Angus – he's not . . . well, I mean, don't get too serious, OK? He's the kind of guy who doesn't like to be tied down.'

'That's cool,' Cleo quipped. 'I'm fresh out of ropes right now. See you! Bye!'

2.00 p.m.
I want to be alone – not

'And you're quite sure you'll be OK on your own?' Holly's mum asked anxiously. 'It's just that there's so much to sort out and you ought to rest.'

'I'll be fine,' Holly said, nodding. 'This room is dead swish – and I've got Sky TV as well. Only –' she paused '– Mum, where's the fire escape?'

Two minutes later . . .

'If you feel ill, phone us,' her mother ordered after showing Holly the plan on the back of the bedroom door, with the list of rules for emergencies clearly typed out. 'See you in a couple of hours.'

The instant her mother shut the door, Holly grabbed the phone by her bed and dialled nine for an outside line. She punched in Cleo's number with her good hand. 'It's me, I'm at the hotel. So what's the plan for tomorrow?' she asked.

'Page eleven – the causes of the Vietnam War,' Cleo replied.

'Oh, parents in sight, yes?' Holly queried.

'That's right,' Cleo said. 'How are you feeling?'

'Not too bad,' Holly said. 'Well, grotty, actually – I don't suppose you fancy coming round?'

'You lost the geography books too? Oh bad luck . . . Mum, I'm just going to drop some school work off at Holly's hotel, OK? Everything got burned up in the fire.' Holly heard Mrs Greenway's muffled agreement in the background. 'See you in about half an hour,' Cleo whispered. 'Loads to tell you.'

The instant Holly replaced the handset, the phone rang again. 'May I speak to Holly, please?'

She was sure she knew the voice but didn't dare believe it. 'It's me. Who's that?'

'Kyle,' he said. 'Look, um – I was wondering if I could pop round to see you? I mean, not if you're too ill.'

'That would be cool,' Holly assured him eagerly. The one upside of smoke damage was a very husky, sexy voice. 'When?'

'Well, to be honest, I'm in the phone box outside the hotel now,' he confessed. 'So about two minutes?'

'OK – it's room 312,' she told him.

Oh God, thought Holly. My hair's a mess, my face is blotchy, I smell of antiseptic and I can't even put lip-gloss on without help. A real turn on I'm going to be. I shall just have to rely on my innate charm. Not.

Ten minutes later . . .

'I'm here because I'm worried about this Cleo and Angus thing,' Kyle burst out after a few minutes of small talk about hospitals and bands. You are meant, thought Holly with a sigh, to be here because of your deep seated craving to spend time with me. 'See, Cleo told me that she and Angus – well, they've got a bit of a thing going,' he went on.

'Do you have a problem with that?' Holly asked, willing him to come up with the right answer.

'Yes, well, no – I don't know.' Kyle shrugged.

'Oh, very decisive,' teased Holly. 'So what are you trying to say?'

'I don't think it'll work out,' he said. 'You're Cleo's mate – you don't want her to get hurt, do you?'

'Of course not,' Holly agreed. 'But why should she? I mean, they're hardly eloping together – they've only had a couple of snogs.'

'But Angus isn't – I mean, he doesn't know – oh hell, this is so hard!' He took a deep breath. 'Angus is what they call confused about his sexuality,' he blurted out, avoiding her gaze. 'He's in a right muddle about it, and frankly, I think he's using Cleo to find out whether he's straight or gay.'

One point to you, Jade Williams, thought Holly, her heart sinking. 'Come off it,' she said 'He didn't seem very uncertain to me. He even chats her up in front of his mother.'

'That,' said Kyle emphatically, 'is half the problem. His parents are homophobic and that's putting it kindly. He'd do anything to have them believe he's what they call normal.'

Holly was aware of the sneer in his voice as he uttered the final word. She took a deep breath. 'And you? You're gay, aren't you?'

Kyle nodded. 'You knew?' he asked. 'So how come you told Cleo you fancied me?'

'Sadly,' Holly said, 'you can fancy someone even when they're not available. You can even kid yourself into believing that they might change.'

'Tell me about it,' Kyle said, sighing. 'So you'll tell Cleo?'

'You can tell her yourself,' Holly informed him. 'She'll be here in a few minutes.'

'Oh no!' Kyle jumped to his feet. 'This is girl-to-girl stuff. Just tell her that Angus is out of bounds, OK?'

'No way,' said Holly. 'I'll tell her what you've told me – but it's up to Angus in the end to work out just who he is. Not us.'

Kyle nodded. 'Just don't let her get in too deep,' he urged. 'Believe me, she'll end up getting hurt. Trust me. I've been there.'

Fifteen minutes later . . .

'This room service idea is cool!' Cleo grinned, as she demolished a mug of hot chocolate and a large slice of carrot cake. 'I can't stop long though. I'm due at Angus's house soon to rehearse. I thought I'd get there a bit early so we can have some time on our own. He is just so cool, Holly, and I really think he likes me.'

'I wanted to talk to you about that,' Holly began tentatively. 'Kyle came round earlier. . .'

'He did? That was all down to me. I told him what you thought about him.'

'I know precisely what you told him,' Holly retorted. 'The thing is, you were wasting your time.'

'How come?' Cleo mumbled through a mouthful of

cake. 'Don't tell me that just as I set you two up, you've gone off him?'

'Cleo, he's gay,' Holly burst out. 'He admitted it in words of one syllable. And Angus . . .'

'Angus is so not gay!' Cleo exploded. 'Gay guys don't come on to you, kiss you, fondle your backside whenever they get the chance.'

'They might if – well, if they weren't sure what they were,' Holly ventured. 'Or if they were scared of coming out.'

'You are so unbelievable!' Cleo raged, her face flushing bright red. 'OK, so Kyle's gay and because you can't have him, you don't want me to be in with a chance with Angus, is that it?'

'No, of course not.' To her surprise, she felt like bursting into tears.

'Well, I'm telling you this. What Angus and I have done together proves he's as straight as the next guy, OK.'

'Done? You haven't?'

'Oh, don't be so dumb. I'm not stupid. But we've snogged big time. Maybe Kyle's miffed because he likes Angus too, but that's not my problem.'

'You could be right,' Holly consented, desperate to keep the peace. 'He did seem pretty uptight about it all. Only he also mentioned that Angus's mum is part of the problem.'

'She's over the moon about us two,' Cleo cut in. 'She even burst in on us when we were kissing and practically applauded!'

Holly opened her mouth and shut it again. Cleo's last remark confirmed everything Kyle had said, but right now she was too tired and too tearful to care. Let

Cleo sort out her own life. Suddenly all she wanted to do was sleep.

3.00 p.m.
More cake and good advice

'I told you that you wouldn't have to take drugs,' Tansy's mum told Andy's mother, as she pushed the double buggy up the hill away from the doctor's surgery.

'He only gave in because you pestered him so much,' Val said with a smile. 'But all that family counselling and transactional analysis stuff he went on about – it makes me feel like we're just a failure as a family.'

'Rubbish!' replied Tansy's mum. 'Failures are people who sit around and do nothing to sort themselves out. You're being as gutsy as anything.'

'And all these herbal tinctures you said you knew about?' Val said, wrinkling her nose. 'You think that they might work? Stop me losing my cool and crying all the time?'

'Passiflora helps you sleep and the other stuff is great when you feel swamped,' Clarity said. 'Mind you, what I'm going to give you right now is pretty good too.'

'Not more weeds and herbs?'

'No, dear,' smiled Tansy's mum. 'A large slice of chocolate layer cake at Betty's Kettle!'

3.55 p.m.

HI! HERE'S MY NEW PHONE NUMBER. GET TXTING!

168

Within seconds of zapping the message to everyone she could think of, Holly's phone shrilled with its new klaxon ring tone.

'Holly, it's Jade! I've been trying to ring you ever since I heard but I couldn't get through.'

'My phone got lost in the fire but this new one is heaps better – it does pictures and everything. How was France? Find any fit Parisien guys?'

'Not Parisien, no,' Jade replied.

'But?'

'Well, there was this guy – oh, I'll tell you all about it when I see you. I'm coming back first thing tomorrow. I want to check you out for myself.'

'That's really nice of you,' Holly told her. 'So you'll be at Rock Hard?'

'No, I thought I'd spend the evening with you – cheer you up for not being able to go.'

'Not going? Course I'm going.' Even as she spoke, Holly's stomach lurched and she tried to push the thought of leaving this safe little bedroom out of her mind. 'Why don't you come over here beforehand? Then we can roll up together?' Or not, as the case may be, she thought.

'OK.'

It occurred to Holly that Jade sounded even less enthusiastic about the whole idea than she was.

4.05 p.m
Nesting instincts

'We've found a house to rent!' Holly's mum cried, bursting into her room. 'It's only two years old, fully furnished and it's just round the corner from Cleo's so that'll be nice for you, won't it?'

'How long will it take to rebuild The Cedars?' Holly asked, pushing the thought of being surrounded by other people's things out of her mind.

'Ah,' said her mother.

'What do you mean, "ah"?'

'We've been talking to the insurance people, and the estate agents and architects and, well, it's early days, but they're suggesting that it's just not a good idea to rebuild.'

'So, where do we go? What do we do?' There was a note of desperation in Holly's voice.

'The insurance money will cover the loss of the house, and we're thinking we might sell the land for redevelopment,' Holly's mum told her. 'It was Mrs Meadows' idea – she'd read this article about developers wanting land in Dunchester. Apparently they could get three or four houses on to a plot that size and our advisers reckon we could get quite a nice sum of money.'

'Enough to buy a nice new house?'

'A very nice one,' her mother assured her. 'So does that make you feel better?'

Holly nodded. 'Just one thing,' she added. 'Can you choose something in the civilised world? No more flats in the middle of nowhere?'

'I'll do my best,' her mother said, laughing. 'But you know your father. He's a law unto himself.'

'It is time,' Holly told her firmly, 'that you took him in hand.'

6.00 p.m.
Rock on!

'Jade? It's Flynn. Listen, when do you get back home?'

'I'm at my gran's now,' Jade told him. 'I'm catching a train home tomorrow morning.'

'Terrific!' he exclaimed. 'Because I've got a bunch of tickets for a rock concert tomorrow in Dunchester and I wondered if you'd like to come. I mean, you've probably got loads on and it's OK but. . .'

'I'd love to,' she cut in. 'You mean Rock Hard, right?'

'Yeah. One of my mates from Phab plays for one of the bands. My dad's dropping me off so we could pick you up on the way, OK?'

'Cool,' she agreed. 'I'll ring you when I get home, yes? Talk later then. Bye!' She stuffed her mobile back in her pocket and jigged round the room, wiggling her bottom and punching the air.

'Good news?' Her gran smiled as she emerged from the kitchen with two mugs of tea.

'It was Flynn,' Jade said.

'That much,' her gran said, laughing, 'I had worked out for myself.'

6.45 p.m.
Hitting the headlines

'You're famouse, darling!' Holly's mum pushed the newspaper in front of her. '*Brave Teen Rescues Tot!*' screamed the headline above a photograph of Holly.

'Where did they get that?' she gasped, eyeing the picture in disgust.

'I gave it to them,' her mum replied proudly. 'You were upset when Leo interviewed you, and he phoned and asked me to find a snapshot.'

'This was taken last year. I look a total dweeb.'

'Don't be silly, darling, you look sweet,' her mother protested.

Holly shook her head in disbelief. 'How could you do this to me? People have been dragged before the Court of Human Rights for less.'

7.00 p.m.
Final rehearsal – and a bit of soul searching

'That sounded great!' Mrs Walker chirped, peering round the basement door as the band finished rehearsing. 'All ready for tomorrow?'

'As good as we'll ever be,' Angus said, slipping his arm round Cleo. 'Now it's down to the fans and the judges.'

'Well, I hope you're packing them in,' his mother said. 'I'm coming, of course, with Dad and Auntie Shirley and . . .'

'Mum, it's not your scene,' Angus protested. 'It's all young people.'

'Nonsense,' his mother declared. 'I want to be there to see my boy give his all. Your parents will be there, I'm sure, won't they, Cleo?'

Over my dead body, thought Cleo. 'No, rock music isn't their scene,' she replied.

'Nor mine,' Mrs Walker sniffed, turning to go up the stairs from the basement. 'But I would always put my boy before my own needs. Then again, we can't all be the same, can we?'

'Coming for a beer?' Kyle asked Angus, clearly eager to change the subject.

'Sure,' he said. 'Liam, are you up for it?'

'When do I ever refuse a drink?' he said, grinning.

'You can't do that,' Angus's mother protested. 'What about Cleo? She's too young to be hanging out in pubs.'

'I'm fine,' Cleo assured her, suppressing the desire to wring the woman's neck for drawing attention to her age. 'I've got to get back anyway.'

'Then Angus will walk you home, won't you, dear?' his mother insisted.

'Well, yes – I mean, if Cleo wants me to,' he stammered, slipping a sweaty hand into hers.

Cleo couldn't help seeing the thunderous look crossing Kyle's face, or the glance he exchanged with Liam.

'That would be nice,' Cleo nodded. 'Thanks.'

'We'll all go,' said Kyle. 'We can have a drink after.'

Sugar, thought Cleo angrily. But what worried her even more was the look of relief on Angus's face.

10.00 p.m.
Bedtime fears

'Holly, it's time you went to sleep,' her mother told her as Holly sat in her parents' bedroom, watching TV. 'Remember what they said at the hospital about taking things easy.'

'Ten more minutes,' Holly pleaded.

'You sound like you did when you were little,' her father teased.

'I feel little,' said Holly and burst into tears. 'I'm scared of going to sleep – what if something awful happens and I don't wake up?'

Ten minutes later . . .

'Now I feel guilty,' Holly said, slipping into her pyjamas and climbing into the double bed beside her mother. 'Do you think Dad minds being on his own in my room?'

'Of course not,' her mum assured her. 'Just for tonight – just till you get your confidence back.'

'Do you think I'll feel normal again soon?' Holly asked, lying back on the pillows. 'I don't even want to go to Rock Hard tomorrow.'

'So don't go,' her mother reasoned.

'Mum!' Holly protested. 'I have to. It's Cleo's big night and . . .'

'It's what?'

'I mean,' Holly gabbled in desperation, 'Cleo's mum only agreed to her going if I was going.'

'Oh, I'm sure I can have a word with Diana and sort that out,' her mother said airily. 'I'll ring her in the morning.'

'No, Mum! No way – promise me. I'll be fine tomorrow, I'm sure I will. Just don't talk to Mrs Greenway, OK?'

Her mother frowned and eyed her closely. 'Are you hiding something from me?' she asked.

'Mum, would I?' Holly gasped. 'Go to sleep.'

SATURDAY

7.30 a.m.
The Vines' hotel suite

'Holly? How long have you been awake?'

Holly's mum yawned and sat up in bed, rubbing her eyes and frowning at Holly, who was sitting in a chair by the window.

'Not long,' Holly lied. If she told her mother she'd been awake since four because she was scared of any more bad dreams, her mum would only worry.

'Right,' her mum declared, throwing back the covers. 'I'm going to change the dressing on your hand. Have you taken your antibiotic?'

Holly nodded. It had occurred to her that it could be the medicine that was making her feel so shaky and weepy. Tansy's mum said drugs of any sort were bad for you – Tansy always got given stewed dandelion or a homeopathic pill if she was ill. Perhaps if she stopped taking the antibiotic, she'd feel more normal again.

'So, are you up to going into town to buy some clothes?' her mother asked, gently unwinding the bandage and peeling off the lint dressing.

'Is the earth round?' Holly grinned. 'I'll phone Tansy and get her to come along – ouch!'

'Sorry,' her mum said. 'I could spare an hour or so, darling, if you'd rather take me.'

Like no, thought Holly. The Spanish Inquisition over skirt lengths and plunging necklines I can do without.

'Don't worry, Mum,' she replied sweetly. 'You've got enough on. I'll be fine.'

9.30 a.m.
Giving in

'Hi, Tansy, it's me, Holly. Can you come shopping with me? I've got all this cash to spend on clothes.' Even as she spoke, she was half praying that Tansy would refuse. It wasn't that she didn't want new clothes; it was simply that suddenly she couldn't muster up any enthusiasm for going out. 'You will? Cool!' The words tripped off her lips, but her heart was beginning to race alarmingly. 'Mum said she'd drop me off. See you by the fountain in the Mall at ten o'clock.'

Holly slumped down on the end of the bed. She didn't get it. One minute she felt fine, the next all she wanted was burst into tears and hide under the bedclothes. It had to be the antibiotics – she taken one an hour before, and that's why she felt so dreadful now. From now on, she'd ditch them. Then she'd be back to old self.

9.55 a.m.
Diversionary tactics

'Good heavens above,' Holly's mum cried as she edged her way through the traffic in Guildhall Road. 'What's with the TV van?'

Holly peered out of the window. A huge lorry marked Anglia TV was parked outside the Riverside Centre, and a couple of guys were wheeling reels of cable across the pavement.

'They must be filming at Rock Hard,' Holly commented. 'Wired are the lead band, you know.' She knew full well that her mother wouldn't have a clue who they were, but with a bit of luck it would shut her up.

'I'll park here,' her mother went on. 'I've got to go to the bank, then I'm off to meet Dad at the estate agent's.'

It was while she was manoeuvring the car into the space that Holly saw the poster advertising Rock Hard. Slapped across the middle of the logo was a fluorescent orange sticker which read: '*Hot News! Local Band Kick-Start Makes the Final! Your Vote Counts.*' Worse was the blown-up photograph of the band that had been slapped onto the bottom of the poster. When her mother opened the car door, the first thing to meet her eyes would be Cleo in the arms of three hunky guys.

Holly pushed open the passenger door, jumped out and leaned against the wall.

'OK, OK,' her mother said with a laugh, pulling on the handbrake and killing the engine. 'I know you're in a hurry to get to the shops.' She locked the car and began striding up the road.

Holly breathed a sigh of relief. Trouble was, when her mum returned to the car would she see the poster? And if she did, would she blurt it all out to Cleo's mum? She toyed with the idea of ripping the poster down off the wall but the street was crowded and it would look highly suspicious. It would be fine. After all, her mum wasn't that observant. And anyway, she didn't have the energy to worry about it.

10.05 a.m.
Early-warning systems go

'Cleo? It's Tansy. Holly and me have some bad news. It's about the Rock Hard posters . . .'

10.07 a.m.
More diversionary tactics

'Mum? You're not going into town today, are you?' Cleo asked anxiously, hovering at her mother's side as she made herself a cup of tea.

'Absolutely not, so if you've got any ideas about me ferrying you here there and everywhere, you can think again,' her mum replied wearily. 'I just want a day of slobbing and doing absolutely nothing.'

'Great idea,' Cleo replied enthusiastically. 'And if you need anything – anything at all – I'll go and get it, OK?'

'That's sweet, darling.' Her mum smiled. 'How thoughtful.'

11.00 a.m.
Panic stations

'Don't Holly thought, relief flooding over her. I feel much better. Which proves it was the tablets. 'How do I look in this?' she asked Tansy, twirling round in a pink cami top and green suede skirt.

'Cool.' Tansy nodded. 'Better still with a pair of those ruched boots like Jade's got. Pay for that lot, and then let's go to FootLoose and check them out.'

It happened without warning. One minute she was

heading along the mall, wondering if she could skimp on her new school uniform and get a fake fur jacket to add to her pile of new clothes; the next she felt as if her throat were closing up, she couldn't breathe and she began sweating as if she'd just run a marathon. She clamped a hand to her throat.

'Holly, are you OK?' Tansy's voice seemed to be echoing from miles away. 'Holly?' She felt Tansy's hand on her arm as she led her to a bench.

She slumped down, panting and clutching at her neck. 'I can't breathe, my throat . . .' she gasped. Then, suddenly, she was crying, great jerking sobs. As she cried, her breathing got easier, and she became aware of Tansy kneeling in front of her, gripping her hands.

'It's OK,' Tansy assured her. 'Just sit still and breathe deeply.'

Holly's hands and lips began tingling and the blood pounded in her head. 'I've got to get out of here,' she gasped, but try as she would she couldn't move. And then, suddenly, the feeling began to fade. Holly swallowed hard. 'It's passing,' she whispered. 'I thought I was going to faint. I couldn't breathe. It was like I was back in the fire.' She closed her eyes and a shiver ran through her body.

Tansy put an arm round her shoulder. 'I'll phone your mum,' Tansy said, taking her phone from her pocket. 'What's her number?'

'Get real,' Holly replied with a weak smile. 'We might as well send the parents a chain letter as let my mother come into town and see these posters. Anyway, I feel a bit better now.'

'Sure?'

Holly nodded. 'It's probably those grotty pills. I sure as hell am not taking any more.' She took a deep breath and stood up. 'Do you think a doughnut would stop my knees shaking?' she asked.

'Sure to.' Tansy smiled. 'And if that doesn't work, we could always try chips.'

11.45 a.m.
Railway station

'Jade darling! Did you have the most marvellous time?' Paula ran along the station platform, enveloped Jade in a big hug and took her suitcase in her hand.

'The car's outside,' she said. 'Now tell me all about it.'

'We went up the Eiffel Tower, and on the river, and I've had my picture painted and we went to Les Printemps and I've got you some dead-smelly cheese . . . Hey, wait! Paula, come here – look!' She pointed to a billboard in the station concourse.

'*Rock Hard*,' she read. '*Local Band, KickStart* – oh my God!' Her mouth dropped open. 'See? That's Cleo – with Kyle and that lot. Remember – they did the disco at my party when . . .' Her voice trailed off.

'I'd rather you didn't remind me about your disastrous party,' said Paula with a wry smile.

'It says here they're through to the final – the final of what?'

Paula shrugged. 'Darling, don't ask me. 'No doubt you'll be on the hotline to Holly and she will know.'

'Oh gosh, I forgot for a moment,' Jade gasped. 'How is she? What about the house? Where are they living?'

'Get in the car, and I'll tell you everything,' her aunt told her. 'Are you going to this Rock thing tonight?'

Jade nodded eagerly. 'Yes, Flynn's dad is picking me up . . .'

'Hang on. Flynn? Who is Flynn?'

'Oh, it's a long story,' Jade faltered.

'So begin,' ordered her aunt. 'Like now.'

Five minutes later . . .
Bending the truth

Paula sighed for the third time. 'I don't know . . . You can't just go off for the evening with a total stranger. I mean, I don't know a thing about him . . .'

'He's really nice, and he's not a stranger – not to me, anyway,' Jade insisted. 'And he's in a wheelchair, which means if I don't go he can't go.' That was, she knew, totally untrue, but it appeared to have the desired effect.

'Well, I suppose it will be all right. Tell you what, I'll have a quick word with Cleo's mum. If she's singing, they're bound to be going and that'll put my mind at rest.'

Jade sighed to herself but said nothing. The Riverside Centre was vast, and she could easily avoid the Greenways. If talking to Cleo's mum was going to calm Paula down, it was worth it.

12 noon
Messing up big time

'Don't you dare make me sound like some wimpish kid!' Jade warned, as Paula pressed the Greenways' doorbell.

'As if!' Paula retorted under her breath as the front

door opened. 'Oh, Diana, sorry to bother you on a Saturday – oh dear, are you ill?'

Jade was surprised to see Cleo's mum in a faded dressing gown, with her hair dishevelled and no make up. She was usually by far the most stylish of all her friends' parents.

'No, just slobbing,' Diana assured her, suppressing a yawn. 'Come in.' She ushered them through to the kitchen, pausing at the foot of the stairs. 'Cleo! Jade's here – can you come down?' She pushed a pile of news-papers to one side of the kitchen table and gestured to them to sit down.

'How was Paris, Jade?' she asked. 'You're back in time for Rock whatever it is tonight, I see!'

'That's what we called about,' Paula interrupted as Cleo burst into the kitchen. 'Jade seems to have picked up this boy . . .'

'Hey, what's this?' Cleo cut in. 'Don't tell me you pulled a French guy?' Jade noticed that Cleo looked impressed.

'No, he's English, and I didn't pick him up,' Jade burst out indignantly, 'I met him on a train.'

'Whatever,' Paula muttered. 'Anyway, Diana, I just thought, that since you'll be going tonight, you'd keep an eye on things.'

She is so embarrassing, Jade thought. What does she think we're going to do?

'What's to keep an eye on?' she insisted, seeing the look of disbelief crossing Cleo's anxious face. 'You're being neurotic.'

'Not neurotic, just careful,' Paula insisted. 'I'm sure Cleo's mum understands.'

'I'm sorry, Paula,' Diana murmured, her expression clearly indicating that she couldn't begin to understand, 'but I won't be going. Frankly, these rock things are not my scene, and besides it's a young people's night, isn't it?'

'Well, yes,' Paula admitted, 'but I thought with Cleo singing with this band, you'd be there cheering her on.'

'It's so cool – you never told me you were singing,' Jade added enthusiastically.

'Nor me,' Cleo's mum stressed, her eyes narrowing as she glared at Cleo.

'I'm not,' Cleo burst out. 'You told me I couldn't sing with the band any more, remember, Mum?'

'But your picture's on those posters,' Jade cut in.

'What posters?' Diana asked sternly.

'Oh, those!' Cleo shrugged. 'The band got through to the finals of this contest, and they had to come up with a photo – that was the only one they had. They could hardly airbrush me out, could they?'

'And this has nothing to do with you? You're just going to watch?' her mother stressed.

'Thanks to you, yes,' Cleo lied.

'That's all right then.' Her mother sighed with relief. She turned to Paula. 'Look, it'll be fine – I don't mind dropping the girls there and fetching them at the end . . .'

'You don't want to do that, Mum!' Cleo cried in alarm.

'It's no trouble,' her mother stressed. 'And if you like, Paula, I'll hang about for a bit and check the place out. Just to put your mind at rest. Now, how about a cup of coffee?'

Cleo shoved Jade out of the kitchen and into the hall. 'Well, thank you so much, Jade Williams!' she hissed. 'You have just wrecked my life.'

'How was I to know?' Jade protested, after Cleo had ranted and raved for five minutes without drawing breath. 'I'm not psychic, you know.'

'I guess. Anyway, you got me into this mess, and you're going to have to get me out of it.'

'And just how am I supposed to do that?' Jade asked.

'I'll think of something,' Cleo replied. 'I haven't spent the last week scheming my way into this final just to go and blow it now.'

3.00 p.m.
End of a dream?

Cleo was experimenting with make-up when she heard a car door slam in the driveway. With a bit of luck, if Jade had got her act together, it would be Holly's mum offering to take Cleo to tea at the hotel before the concert. She went over to the window and peered out. What she saw made her heart miss a beat.

Angus's mum was climbing out of her four-wheel drive and heading for the front door. Cleo hurled her mascara onto the dressing table and flew down the stairs, wrenching the front door open just as Mrs Walker's finger pressed the bell.

'Hi, Mrs Walker,' she whispered, just in case her mother was within earshot.

'Don't look so worried, dear,' said Mrs Walker. 'Nothing's wrong.'

Apart from the fact you're here, thought Cleo, just as Roy's study door opened and his balding head peered out. 'Cleo, who is it?' he called.

'You must be Cleo's father.' Mrs Walker beamed broadly and stepped into the hall, the bangles on her wrist jangling as she stretched out a hand to Roy.

'Her stepfather, actually,' Roy corrected her. 'And you are?'

'Angus's mother,' Mrs Walker told him.

'Angus?' Roy frowned.

'One of my mates,' Cleo gabbled.

'Oh, rather more than a mate, I think,' giggled Angus's mum. 'Which is why I'm here. I thought to myself, if the two young ones are getting so close, it's time us oldies did the same!'

'I'm sorry, but you really have lost me,' Roy began looking a little impatient. 'But perhaps my wife . . .'

As he spoke, Diana came down the stairs. 'I thought I heard voices,' she said, looking enquiringly from Roy to Mrs Walker and back again.

'This is Mrs Walker,' Cleo said with a sigh, giving up all hope of saving the day.

'Oh my goodness – not the Walkers who were going to buy Angela Vine's house?' Cleo's mum said. 'What a dreadful business that was.'

'I know, and a lucky escape for us – I mean, fancy putting a house on the market with dodgy wiring. We might have found all sorts of other things wrong, and as I said to my husband –'

'What can we do for you?' Diana cut in firmly.

Mrs Walker put her hand in her coat pocket and waved two tickets in the air. Cleo's heart plummeted straight through the floorboards.

'Cleo said rock music wasn't your scene, but I

thought it would be fun if you came along tonight with my husband and me,' she said. 'If we want to see our kids on TV, we must encourage them, don't you agree?'

'TV?' Diana's voice came out as a high pitched squeak.

'And every vote counts – we might just tip the balance between the band winning and losing.'

For a moment you could have heard a pin drop in the Greenways' hall. Then all hell exploded.

'I don't know,' Roy declared, 'quite what Cleo has been telling you but she is not going anywhere with any band, tonight or at any other time.'

'What do you mean?' Mrs Walker gasped. 'You can't be saying . . .'

'I'm saying that Cleo was strictly forbidden from getting mixed up with all this band nonsense.' He spun round to face his wife. 'Diana, I suppose you were in on all this?'

Cleo's mum shook her head. 'Certainly not.' She turned to Cleo. 'You told me only hours ago that you weren't involved.' The disappointment in her mother's voice affected Cleo far more than all her stepfather's ranting and raving. 'I trusted you.'

Mrs Walker stared at Cleo, open-mouthed. 'You mean,' she asked, 'you hadn't told your parents? They knew nothing about it?'

'Only because they said I couldn't sing with the band any more, and Angus really wanted me to, and I didn't want to let him down,' she gabbled.

'Oh, and you think dropping out four hours before the final is being fair?' Mrs Walker demanded.

'It's not my idea to drop out,' Cleo reasoned, close to tears.

'Perhaps,' Cleo's mum suggested, 'we could make an exception, just for tonight.'

'The hell we can!' Roy stormed. 'I'm sorry, Mrs Walker, but we have to stand firm on this. What if they win, and Cleo gets caught up in all that virtual TV rubbish?' Mrs Walker opened her mouth to speak, but Roy was unstoppable. 'Now if you will excuse us, I think we need some time on our own to sort things out.' He opened the front door and practically pushed Angus's mum on to the step.

'I really thought,' she said, turning and holding Cleo's gaze, 'that you were the sort of girl I'd be proud to see out with my son. I was wrong.' She took a deep breath. 'I suppose I had better go home and break the news to him. It's not just the band, you know. You're the first girl he's been really keen on, and I wouldn't be at all surprised if you haven't broken his heart. Thank you for nothing.'

Two minutes later . . . Retribution

'How could you act in such a despicable, underhand way?' Roy snorted, the hairs in his nostrils waving indignantly. 'After everything I said to you. Have you no respect?'

'Why should I?' Cleo stormed back, choking back tears. 'You're hardly a role model, are you? It's OK for you to lie and to keep secrets but when I do it, you come on the oh-so-perfect parent.'

'Cleo, that's not fair. Roy doesn't lie,' her mother cut in.

'Oh really? So ask him just where he's been these last

few days. Ask him why we can never reach him on the phone. Ask him about his job!'

'Cleo, for God's sake, you promised . . .' Roy began.

'She promised what, Roy?' Diana's voice was tinged with panic. 'What's going on?'

'I've had a bit of trouble at work,' Roy muttered.

'What sort of trouble?'

'Nothing for you to worry about,' he hesitated. 'Just a bit of departmental reorganisation.'

'And you say that I tell lies?' Cleo stormed. 'He's lost his job, Mum. He's been conning you into thinking he's at the office every day.'

Diana sank down on to one of the kitchen stools, her face draining of colour. Cleo felt a pang of conscience as Roy went to her side and took her hand. 'You've done what?' Cleo's mum shrugged Roy's hand away. 'I don't understand. Why didn't you tell me?' she asked in disbelief. 'Didn't you think I had a right to know?'

'How could I tell you?' Roy mumbled. 'You've been so down in the dumps and I just thought it would make you worse.'

'But surely you knew I'd find out eventually?'

'I thought I'd get a new job really quickly and then it would be fine,' he said. 'I didn't want you to worry.'

'Which is exactly why I didn't tell you about the TV thing,' Cleo cut in. 'I thought that if we won and got on TV, you'd be proud of me and if we didn't win – well, there was no point having a row and upsetting you.'

'What is it with you two?' her mother exploded. 'Do you think I'm some neurotic middle-aged woman who needs to be treated like a kid? OK, so I've been low lately

– but I can tell you one thing: I feel a damned sight worse knowing you've both lied to me.'

'I didn't mean . . .' Roy and Cleo began together.

'Cleo, a few weeks back, I actually asked you to come on that mum and daughter show on TV with me and you refused – said you couldn't hack it. So what's changed?'

'Angus . . .'

'I might have guessed,' Roy cut in, 'that some boy was behind all this.'

'What's with all the shouting?' Cleo's little sister, Lettie, peered round the door carrying her riding hat and crop. 'You're not getting a divorce, are you?'

'Don't be silly, of course we're not,' Roy replied.

'Good,' said Lettie. 'So what's going on?'

'They're just busy messing up my life,' said Cleo, as her phone bleeped. 'And once they've done that, they'll probably start on yours.'

She glanced at her phone and burst into tears.

HOW COULD U DO THIS 2 US? U R LETTING US ALL DOWN. RING ME. ANGUS.

Her mother grabbed the phone, read the message, and thrust it back at Cleo. 'Right,' she said. 'What time does this thing begin?'

'Seven o'clock. Why?' Cleo sniffed.

'Text him and say you'll be there,' her mother ordered.

'Diana, what are you thinking of?' Roy burst out. 'Are you going against my express wishes?'

'Yes,' his wife replied. 'But at least I'm being open about it.'

Five minutes later . . . Promises, promises

'Thanks, Mum,' Cleo said for the third time, after Roy had left the room to answer the phone. 'I promise I'll never lie to you again.'

'You'd better not,' warned her mother. 'And don't think you won't be punished for lying. The only reason I'm letting you go is because I'm a professional and I happen to believe that the show must go on.'

'OK.'

'After tonight, you're grounded for a fortnight.'

'OK.'

'And I'm taking you and fetching you – and I might even hang around to hear you.'

'OK.'

'And if you win and get into this TV show, they'll have to find another lead singer. GCSEs are more . . .'

'OK.'

'Come on, give me a hug. I think we could both do with one.'

Recriminations

'So you've given in to her yet again,' Cleo heard Roy mumble from behind the closed sitting room door. 'My word means nothing in this house.'

'I'm meeting her halfway,' her mother replied. 'She gets to go tonight because too many people will be let down if she doesn't.' Cleo heard her stepfather grunt sarcastically. 'And now, about your job,' her mother went on. 'What are we going to do?'

'We?' Roy sighed. 'It's down to me to deal with.'

'Don't be so daft,' Cleo's mum replied. 'We're in this together. I'll cash in my ISA and that'll keep us going for a few months. And first thing on Monday I'm going to start looking for a regular job. And that's a promise.'

What Cleo couldn't understand was that her mum sounded more positive than she had in weeks.

Meanwhile, in the hotel . . .

'So as a friend, thought Holly, as her mother picked up the in-house phone and dialled the Greenways' number. Cleo will kill me.

'Holly, go to your room,' her mother ordered. 'I don't want you butting in every five seconds while I'm talking to Diana.'

'Mum, do you have to?' Holly tried for one final reprieve. 'I really want to go.' Sort of.

'Holly – out. Now.'

Holly ambled out of the room and paused in the corridor. Sticking her foot out so that the door didn't close properly, she strained her ears to catch what her mother was saying.

'Diana, is that you? Holly's mum here,' her mother burst out. 'Look, I know you said Cleo couldn't go to the concert unless Holly went, but between you and me, I don't think Holly's up to it, although of course, she's denying it, and – what? Cleo's singing? What band? Good heavens above!'

There was a long pause before her mother began speaking again. 'That's obviously why Holly's so keen to go, but she never said a word about Cleo taking part. You didn't know either? Honestly, kids!'

6.00 p.m.
Painful parents

'You're early!' Tansy gasped as her mum let Andy into the cottage. 'I'm not ready.'

'I needed to get out of the house.'

'Your parents aren't arguing again, are they?' Tansy asked, beckoning to him to follow her up the stairs.

He shook his head. 'No, Dad's gone into silent mode, and Mum's rushing round trying to be extra nice,' he said. 'It's a real role reversal – she's usually the moody one.'

'Maybe he doesn't like this idea of counselling,' Tansy ventured. 'Not sure I would.'

'Counselling?' Andy asked. 'What counselling?'

'That's what gets me about parents,' Andy said, sighing, after Tansy had admitted that her mother had told her all about the visit to the doctor. 'They expect us to tell them every single thing that happens in our lives and then they clam up and shut us out. When do you think they start realising we're adults?'

'Round about our fortieth birthdays, I guess.' Tansy grinned as she fingered styling gel through her flyaway hair. 'Personally, I find it's best to carry on regardless.' She touched his arm. 'She'll get over it, you know,' she assured him.

'It's not the bloody flu,' Andy snapped.

'OK, no need to take it out on me,' Tansy retorted.

'Sorry,' Andy began.

'Although,' Tansy went on with a smile, 'I'd far

rather you took it out on me than than you disappeared again. Deal?'

'Deal.' Andy nodded, and kissed her.

7.05 p.m.
This is it

'Cleo! Over here!' Angus waved wildly from the middle of the crush of people backstage at the Riverside Centre. 'Thank God you came. What was all that about?'

'You don't want to know,' Cleo assured him. 'Have you got the running order? When are we on?'

'Third,' Kyle cut in. 'Best place really – two bands ahead of us to warm the place up, and we're near enough to the end to be remembered. We hope.' He touched Angus's arm. 'You OK? Sorry I yelled earlier. Pre-gig nerves, I guess. And the worry about madam here not turning up.'

Cleo opened her mouth in protest and then thought better of it.

Angus moved closer to Kyle. 'I was jangly too,' he admitted, giving him a friendly dig. 'Truce?'

'What do you think?' Kyle's smile could have lit up a room.

Cleo suddenly felt as if she was invisible. There was something about the easy banter between Angus and Kyle that was completely at odds with the anxious, nervous way he behaved with her. She had a horrible feeling that Holly and Jade were right. But there was only one way to find out, and maybe this evening was as good a time as any. All she had to do was wait for the right moment.

7.10 p.m.
Meet the new Jade

'This is Flynn,' Jade said eagerly, as Holly and the others caught up with them in the area reserved for wheelchairs.

Holly eyed the dark-skinned guy with the amazing eyes and wondered how it was that her mates always managed to cream off the fit ones. 'And this is Joe, this is Tamsin and –' she turned to tall girl with long black hair '– sorry, I've forgotten your name.'

'Sumitha,' the girl said. 'Hi.'

Holly hadn't seen Jade looking so bubbly since she dumped Scott. 'So where did you meet all this lot?' Holly hissed at her, as one of the guest bands struck up and Flynn wheeled himself closer to the stage. Tansy and Andy were walking back to their seats, but somehow the thought of sitting in a crush of people made Holly feel sick. The wide open space set aside for wheelchairs seemed a whole lot safer.

'Flynn goes to this club – Phab, it's called,' explained Jade. 'That stands for . . .'

'Physically Handicapped Able-Bodied,' Holly cut in. 'I know – my friend Paul's cousin goes to one.'

'I'm going to join,' Jade added. 'Flynn's going to organise it.'

'You don't mean? You're not, like, an item? But he's in a wheelchair.'

'So?' retorted Jade. 'He's just a friend and anyway, being a member of Phab would make my CV for nursing college look extra good.'

'And it has nothing to do with how good Flynn looks?' Holly replied. 'Get real.'

8.45 p.m.
Behind the scenes

Backstage was frenetic, with guys shifting drum kits and music stands, lighting gear and amplifiers. It was Holly who spotted the band first, largely because her eye was drawn to a large figure in a familiar scarlet cape.

'Oh no, Angus's mum has turned up. And she's dragged Cleo's mum with her. This could be interesting.'

'Now go out there and give it your all,' they heard Mrs Walker insist as they got within earshot. 'Those first two bands weren't a patch on you – with a bit of luck, you'll make the TV show, no problem.' She turned to Cleo's mum. 'And then, won't we be proud?' she chortled.

'Actually,' Cleo's mum cut in, 'there is one thing I have to make quite clear. Regardless of whether they win or lose, I can't allow Cleo . . .'

Holly saw the look of horror crossing Cleo's face and went for it. 'Mrs Greenway,' she murmured. 'I feel . . . I feel dreadful. I think I might be going to faint.'

'Oh, my dear child!' Diana gasped. 'Quick, someone – get her a chair. Water – we need a bottle of water.'

'Put your head between your knees,' ordered Jade. 'We did fainting at St John last month.' Jade shoved Holly's head towards her lap. 'Now keep calm and breathe deeply,' she ordered.

'Attention please! KickStart on stage in three minutes.'

'That's us!' Cleo cried. 'Come on, guys.'

'Good luck!' Tansy and Andy chorused.

'Good luck,' whispered Holly in what she hoped was the voice of one about to expire.

'Go for it,' Mrs Walker shouted.

'Are you sure you're OK, Holly?' Cleo murmured, touching her shoulder as she passed.

Holly winked at her. 'Fine,' Holly hissed. 'But get on stage – I can't keep up this charade for ever.'

In the limelight

'And now I've changed / Directions rearranged . . .'

Get it together, Cleo told herself sternly. She knew she wasn't firing on all cylinders; the resonance had gone out of her voice, and she sounded monotone and bland.

'So don't hang around no-oh-more / Don't come back, I'm right on track and I don't want to hear about you-oooo'

An image of Kyle and Angus gazing at one another backstage swam before her eyes. She's been a fool and she knew it.

'I've seen the light, and it's all right . . .'

They would kill her if they won and she wasn't allowed to sing with them. It might be better if they lost.

'There's nothing you can do / Cos I've changed my direction too!'

Then again, that wasn't fair. Come on, go for it, she told herself. At least you can do that for them.

'I looked back, couldn't relax, red eyes full of anger / Life a mess, only stress,'

That was better. She'd show them. She took a deep breath and let it rip.

Post-mortem

'Gimme five!' Angus slapped Kyle's hand.

'Good or what?' Liam grinned.

'You were a bit shaky at first, Cleo,' Angus said. 'But then – wow, you were a star.'

'And your drumming,' Kyle said, turning to Angus, 'was ace. As ever.'

Cleo couldn't help noticing the look that passed between them.

'Well done, boys!' Angus's mother came through the stage door and bustled over to them. 'And you, of course, Cleo. Not as good as usual but the boys carried you nicely.'

Angus slipped an arm round Cleo and gave her a squeeze. 'She was a star,' he protested, kissing her forehead.

That's when Cleo saw the pain in Kyle's eyes. She turned away. 'I'm going out front to see my mates,' she said, desperately trying to keep the shake out of her voice. 'See you later.'

'Hang on, we'll come too,' Angus called, but she ignored him. If ever she needed proof that Angus was playing a part, she had it now.

9.30 p.m.
Moment of reckoning – in more ways than one

'And remember, your votes count!' The compere from TV-K had taken the stage.

'Our panel of judges have made their decision, but you can change all that. Just five more minutes of voting time and then we'll know who's for the big time!'

Five more minutes, thought Holly, then we can go home. The heat in the auditorium was really getting to her; her head ached and even though she tried to join in the chat with her friends, she kept losing the thread of the conversation.

'So let's bring the bands back on stage for the big moment!' the compere announced.

Spontaneous Combustion came first, followed by Maximum Penalty and then Cleo leading KickStart. The other three bands came on stage from the opposite side amidst cheers and foot stamping.

'Go, go, KickStart!' shouted Tansy, and the others all joined in. 'Go, go, KickStart!'

'Our judges were very impressed with all six bands, but when we put their votes and the votes of you, the audience, together, the winners were . . .'

Tansy gripped Holly's good hand.

'Spontaneous Combustion!'

'Oh no!' Andy thumped a fist against his thigh.

'That is so not on,' muttered Tansy.

The auditorium burst into cheers and applause as Spontaneous Combustion took centre stage, punching the air and hugging one another. Suddenly there was a whoosh and a splutter and great flashes of light as a line of fireworks exploded at the front of the stage.

'No, no . . .' Holly gasped, clutching at Tansy's sleeve. '*No!*' She began edging backwards, her eyes fixed on the multi-coloured explosions in front of her. 'Get me out of here!' she panted. 'Can't breathe, help me, no, no . . .' She felt someone's arm round her shoulder, heard a voice repeating her name from a long, long way away.

'Holly, it's OK, it's just the fireworks.' Tansy's voice sounded as if someone had tuned a radio in badly.

'Can't . . . no . . . please!' Holly felt a cold sweat sweep over her and the faster she panted, the more her lips and face began tingling.

'Come on, we'll go outside.' Cleo's mum was suddenly standing beside her, gripping her arm. 'This way.'

Holly edged backwards, trying to focus on Mrs Greenway's calm voice. But she didn't take her eyes off the stage. She didn't dare. She couldn't risk it. If she did, she'd die. She knew she would.

'Panic attack,' the St John Ambulance guy on duty repeated to Cleo's mum. 'Suffers from claustrophobia, does she?'

'She was in a house fire a few days back,' Cleo's mum told him, stroking Holly's hand as her breathing eased. 'I think the fireworks must have triggered a flashback. She rescued her nephew, you know.'

'The kid in the paper?' the guy exclaimed. 'I read about that. Brave girl, aren't you?'

'I feel a fool,' Holly muttered. 'Did people notice? Me making a fuss, I mean?'

'Apart from Tansy, they were all too wired up about the band result,' Mrs Greenway replied. 'Don't worry. We'll get you home right away. I've sent Tansy to fetch the others.'

'No, I can't spoil it for them,' Holly protested. 'I'll be OK.'

'OK you are not,' said Cleo's mum firmly. 'Do as you're told.'

'You sound like my mum,' Holly said, smiling. And was very pleased about it.

9.40 p.m.
Backstage, feeling gutted

'It was all my fault,' Cleo muttered dejectedly. 'That first bit of the song – I did it all wrong.'

'It was all of us,' Kyle told her. 'We just weren't good enough, that's all.'

'Get real,' Cleo said, 'you've been telling one another how great you were for the last half-hour. It was me and I know it.'

'Cleo's right,' Angus cut in. 'She didn't have her heart in it like she usually does.'

He might as well have stabbed her in the guts with a sharp knife. She couldn't believe he wasn't even looking at her as he spoke or that he was too thick to realise why she'd been preoccupied.

'That's not fair,' Liam began, but broke off as Angus's mother came bursting through the stage door.

'Those judges were rubbish!' she cried, so loudly that several people turned to stare. 'Quite frankly, I think we should appeal.'

'Mum, for heaven's sake . . .' Angus broke in.

'I mean, at least you had a singer, even if she wasn't quite up to her usual . . .' She pulled a face at Angus, as he slipped his arm round Cleo's shoulders. 'Sorry, shouldn't say that about your girlfriend, should I?' she tittered.

Whether it was disappointment or anger, or just brain dead weariness, she didn't know, but Cleo forgot all about good manners and being discreet and just let rip.

'Mrs Walker, I am not Angus's girlfriend,' she snapped, pushing him away from her. 'I don't think Angus even

200

wants a . . .' She paused. She couldn't drop him in it, not here in a public place. And besides, it wasn't up to her. It was something he had to sort out with his own family. '. . . I don't think he wants anything to distract him from his music right now,' she finished, aware of the admiring glance from Kyle. 'And frankly, he's not my type. Now, if you don't mind, I'm going to join my mates.'

It wasn't till the fire door between the stage and the auditorium swung shut behind her that she allowed herself to cry.

10.15 p.m.
Regrets

'I feel so stupid,' Holly said with a sigh as they all squeezed into Mrs Greenway's car.

'You feel stupid?' Cleo retorted. 'You're brave and gutsy, I'm just one dumb idiot. I should have listened to Jade in the first place.'

'Talking of Jade,' Holly added, trying to distract attention from herself, 'what do you think about her and that Flynn guy getting it together?'

'Jade? Seriously involved?' Cleo questioned. 'No way – I guess she's with him because she likes looking after people. He's disabled, after all.'

'Not disabled enough to stop him giving her a lip-to-lip snog marathon.'

'They didn't?'

'Oh yes they did!' Tansy laughed. 'We tried saying goodbye three times and then gave up. They're probably still at it now!'

Meanwhile . . .

'Your dad will be waiting outside,' Jade murmured, gently running her fingers through Flynn's hair.

'True.' He nodded.

'So we'd better get going,' she suggested, not moving an inch.

'I thought we had,' he said, smiling. 'But I'd better just check.'

As his lips touched hers, she realised that perhaps being normal wasn't so hard after all.

SUNDAY

10.00 a.m.
Being thankful

'. . . And please, God, can we find a proper new house so we don't have to live in someone else's, and could you stop my hand hurting and please make the panic attacks go away because I'm really scared.'

Holly opened one eye and gazed at the stained-glass window immediately behind the choir stalls, where Cleo was sitting, looking unusually angelic in a blue cassock and white surplice. She wasn't quite sure whether she really believed that God could hear prayers – after all, with around three million people yabbering at Him at any one time, how could he concentrate on them all? But her RE teacher assured everyone that no problem was too small for him – and if ever Holly needed to put Him to the test it was now.

Even here with her mum on one side of her and her father on the other, she felt nervous and edgy. She kept looking over her shoulder to check that nothing was happening that she couldn't see. She didn't often come to church but at breakfast that morning, her dad had insisted.

'We've got so much to be thankful for,' he told her. 'You and William safe, friends rallying round, and now someone interested in buying The Cedars . . .'

'What?' Holly had burst out. 'It's a wreck.'

'True,' her mum had interrupted. 'But the agent phoned while you were out last night – Conrad Homes are definitely interested in the land and they'll demolish the house. There's a lot to be sorted, but they seem really keen.'

'Which,' her father had carried on, 'is great because I've spotted a place I think would be perfect for us – and with a bit of luck we can afford it.' Holly's mum had looked excited.

'Where? What is it? You never told me . . .' she began.

'It's an old Methodist chapel, fascinating history . . .'

'Dad!'

'Rupert, really!'

'What?' Holly's dad frowned. 'What have I said?'

Remembering his protests, Holly decided something had to be done. 'Oh, and one other thing,' Holly prayed, 'Get my father into the twenty-first century, could you? For all our sakes. Amen.'

11.00 p.m.
Explosive Encounters

'Right,' get the door, there's a dear – I'm just repotting this begonia.'

Tansy ambled to the front door, toast and honey in hand.

'Is your mother in?' Andy's mum was on the doorstep, red-faced and unsmiling.

'Mum, it's Mrs Richards,' Tansy called. 'Come in – Mum's through there.'

Andy's mum pushed past Tansy and marched into the kitchen.

'Val! How are you?' Clarity cried, wiping her hands on her apron and pushing her pot plants to one side. 'Come in, I'll put the kettle on.'

'Never mind all that,' Andy's mum snapped. 'How could you, Clarity? How could you do it?'

'Do what?' Tansy's mum looked bewildered.

'Break a confidence, blab to Tansy about what the doctor said,' shouted Andy's mum. 'And as for you – ' she glared at Tansy '– what possessed you to tell Andy everything? Now he's asking all sorts of awkward questions.'

'Stop right there!' Tansy's mum exploded. 'Let's get a few things straight. One, it was Andy who confided in Tansy because he was worried sick about you. Two, Tansy cared enough to take on board what he was saying and realise you needed help. And three, I told Tansy because I knew she wanted to be there for Andy.' She touched her friend's shoulder. 'It's called supporting your friends,' she concluded.

'But now the whole world is going to know,' Andy's mum protested. 'We'll be known as the family in therapy.'

'That's so not true!' Tansy blurted out. 'We're fifteen, Mrs Richards, not a couple of stupid kids who don't know how to keep their mouths shut.'

Andy's mum ran a hand wearily through her hair. 'I'm sorry,' she murmured. 'I've done it again, haven't I? Messed up like I always do.' She looked at Clarity, her eyes full of tears. 'How come you're always so sensible?'

Tansy laughed. 'Come off it,' she teased. 'My mum could win awards for being daft.'

12.00 noon

'Can we talk, Mum?' Holly asked as they waited to be served in the café.

'Of course, darling – what's up?' her mother asked.

'I'm scared,' Holly admitted. 'Really scared.'

'What of, exactly?'

'Everything,' Holly blurted out. 'That's the problem – it's so stupid. Like last night – I was fine one minute and then suddenly I couldn't breathe and I felt sick and what if . . .?' She hesitated, tearing her paper napkin into shreds. 'What if it happens at school?'

Her mum took her hand. 'You've been through an awful lot, Holly,' she pointed out. 'Everyone understands.'

'Oh like sure!' Holly burst out. 'You don't know the half of it. If I make an idiot of myself once, there are some people who'll make sure no one ever forgets. Do I have to go back to school tomorrow?'

Her mother hesitated. 'I'd love to say you could stay off,' her mum said. 'But I just think that's going to make it worse when the time comes to go back.'

Holly struggled not to cry. 'I thought when I stopped taking the tablets, I'd be fine, but I'm not,' she admitted.

'Do you mean to tell me you haven't been taking your antibiotic?' her mother exclaimed. 'Since when?'

'Only since yesterday when I went all funny at the shops,' Holly said. 'But my hand is throbbing like crazy so I guess I ought to.'

'You are a silly dumpling,' her mother replied affectionately. 'Panic attacks happen when you've been through an ordeal. Not to everyone, but believe me, to far many more people than you would imagine. The pills won't have anything to do with it.' She squeezed Holly's arm. 'You take one right now,' she insisted. 'And as for school, Miss Partridge phoned me while you were out last night. She saw your photo in the paper.'

'Did you tell her about all the work I'd lost? What did she say?'

'She said there was nothing that couldn't be sorted,' her mum told her. 'And I mentioned that you were still a bit shaky, and she suggested you did mornings only for a bit.'

'Like, no!' Holly protested. 'That way I'd miss art – that's always in the afternoons. Besides, I might miss out on the gossip at lunch time and I'd feel even more of a dweeb.'

'I rather think,' her mum said with a grin, 'that you are already on the mend. Just take it easy and don't be too hard on yourself, OK. Now how about getting Tansy, Cleo and Jade over for supper?'

'They probably want to avoid me.' Holly sighed. 'They had to leave early last night because of me.'

'Well, after lunch, phone them and see,' her mother suggested. 'And in the meantime, let's order – you need to keep your strength up.'

1.30 p.m.
Time for a change

'Right,' said Cleo's mother as she carried a dish of roast potatoes to the table. 'Family conference time.' She passed the carving knife and fork to Roy. 'You carve, I'll talk,' she ordered. 'I would have said something at breakfast, but I wanted to wait till Portia got back because this affects us all. I'm going to start teaching speech and drama.'

'Great idea!' Roy exclaimed, almost dropping the carvers in surprise. 'Why didn't you think of that before?'

'But Mum,' Portia interjected, 'don't you have to have qualifications?'

'Probably,' her mother admitted blithely, 'but I reckon that an advert saying that *Diana Greenway, late of the Royal Shakespeare Company* . . .'

'That was twenty years ago,' Roy murmured, passing a plate of roast chicken to Cleo.

'. . . *and well-known TV actress,*' continued Cleo's mum, ignoring him totally, 'should bring them running.'

'So which drama school are you going to teach at?' Cleo asked, knowing full well that her mother was great on ideas and rather less brilliant at the detail.

'None,' her mother said triumphantly, spooning carrots on to her plate. 'I'm going to teach from home.'

'But . . .'

'Enjoy your lunch,' Diana said with a smile. 'Because after tomorrow, this won't be a dining room. It will be called Studio One. Peas, anyone?'

1.45 p.m.
Get real!

'You snogged him?' Allegra stared at her cousin, her mouth open wide.

'Don't sound so surprised,' Jade said, smiling. 'It's not like I've never had a boyfriend before. There was Scott...'

She paused, realising that it might be a tad tactless to tell Legs, who was now going out with her ex-boyfriend, just how hands-on they got in the past.

'Yes, but this guy's disabled,' Allegra butted in. 'You won't be able to go to discos, or hang out in town or anything.'

'Get real. I'm going to a party with him next week, he's going to teach me archery, and his dad said he'd take us out in his boat in the summer. Besides, I don't care what we do. I just want to be with him.'

'Wow!' Allegra grinned. 'You've really fallen big time, haven't you? You've actually joined the real world.'

Jade said nothing. She hadn't agreed with Allegra in the two years she'd lived with her. She saw no need to start now.

2.45 p.m.
Cards on the table time

'Cleo, Angus is here to see you.' Cleo's mum stuck her head round the bedroom door while Cleo was on the phone to Holly.

'Hang on, Holly,' she muttered into her phone. 'Tell him I'm busy, Mum. I really don't want to see him.'

'Just because you're not doing gigs with them any more, doesn't mean you can't show good manners,' her mother told her firmly. 'Just don't agree to sing, OK?'

'Can I go to Holly's for supper?' she asked quickly. One deal deserved another.

'Have you finished your homework?'

'Of course,' Cleo said. Not.

'OK, then, but not too late. School tomorrow.'

'I can come,' Cleo told Holly. 'Got to go now, though. Catch you later.'

Cleo ambled downstairs. Angus was standing in the hall and despite everything she had told herself about him, she couldn't help noticing how fit he looked in his ski jacket and jeans.

'Hi,' he said awkwardly. 'Can we talk?'

'What's to say?' Cleo murmured, ushering him into the sitting room.

'I'm sorry,' he gabbled. 'I'm a coward and an idiot, and I shouldn't have come on to you the way I did.' He looked so embarrassed that Cleo's heart began to melt.

'It's OK,' she said. 'I was dumb too – one of my mates warned me that you weren't into girls. I just chose to ignore her.'

'It's not as easy as that,' Angus burst out. 'I don't know what I am, who I am – the only thing I do know is that I can't be what my parents want. And I don't think I can be what Kyle wants me to be.'

Cleo's heart finished melting. 'Can't you talk to them – say what you've just said to me?'

'I keep telling myself I will,' he admitted. 'It's just that they – well, Mum especially – pin all their hopes on me. You've got no idea what it's like being an only child – parental pressure in spades, all the time. And Kyle's great except that. . .why can't people just leave you alone to get on with life your way? Sort yourself out in your own time?

Cleo nodded. 'I guess,' she said, suddenly feeling very wise and grown up, 'that you have to just start doing things your way and hope they'll cotton on in the end.'

'Does that work for you?'

'I wish,' she said, sighing. 'But with parents, you just have to keep trying.'

Meanwhile, back at the hotel . . .

'Hi, Jade,' Holly said, turning up the volume on her phone in an attempt to drown out the television. 'Yes, I'm feeling much better thanks. You can come? Brilliant.' She gave her mum the thumbs up sign. 'Listen, Ben wants your phone number,' Jade told her, 'but I thought I ought to ask you first.'

'Who's Ben?' Holly frowned.

'You remember, Flynn's mate – the one who was at the concert. He thought you were cool.'

'He did? He clearly doesn't get out much,' Holly laughed.

'Well, shall I pass your number on or not?'

Do I tell her I can't even remember what the guy looks like? Holly thought. What if he saw me having the panic attack and just wants to poke fun at me?

'I told him about the fire and everything and said you might not feel up to being sociable, and he was OK about that because he was in a car crash last year and he said it takes ages to feel like the world is safe.'

'He did?'

'Yes, so I'll tell him not to call you yet, OK?'

'No way,' said Holly. 'He sounds just the kind of guy I thought didn't exist. Give him my number. Like now.'

And back at Cleo's place . . .

'Cleo, come here. Now.'

Cleo's heart sank at the tone of her mother's voice. 'What have I done now?' she said, stomping into the kitchen.

'I've had a phone call about you,' her mother said sternly. 'About last night.'

Cleo racked her brains to think of anything remotely bad she had done in the last twenty-four hours.

'He was at Rock Hard and he said . . .' She burst out laughing. 'Oh, it's no good,' she said, giggling. 'I can't keep a straight face. Darling, it was a man called Vaughan Tyler. He's from the Royal College of Music and he heard you sing last night. He wants to train you!'

Cleo's mouth dropped open.

'Of course, I told him right away that his fees would be way out of our league, especially now, and you know what he said? He'll teach you for a year for just half of the usual fee and see how you get on.'

'That's amazing!' Cleo's face fell. 'Have you told Roy?'

'Not yet, he's been on the phone for hours.'

'Well, I can tell you now that he won't let me do it.'

'Oh yes he will!' The kitchen door swung open and Roy leaned against the doorpost, newspaper in hand. 'I've been a miserable old sod lately and I rather think I need to do something to redeem myself.' Roy gave the odd twitch of the lips that passed for a smile. 'Well done, Cleo – you go for it.'

'Darling!' exclaimed her mother. 'Thank you so much – I guess this means you got the lecturing job with the Judy woman.'

She made it sound as though he was seeking employment with the wicked witch of the east.

'No, I didn't,' Roy replied with a sigh. 'To be honest, I think she was all talk. But there are a lot of management consultancy posts in here –' he tapped the newspaper '– and I'll just have to keep on trying till something turns up,' he concluded. 'And if I'm too old, I'll have to become a house husband while you teach.'

'It won't come to that,' Cleo cried in alarm. Happy as she was right now, the thought of Roy at home 24/7 was more than the human frame could stand.

7.30 p.m.

'Dad says we can order anything we like,' Holly announced as the four of them sat down at a corner table in the hotel's coffee shop. 'But before we start I've got to say something and if I don't say it now, I'll chicken out.' She took a deep breath. 'You know last night, when I had that panic attack and you all had to come home early because of me. Well, I'm really sorry.'

'I'm glad – I mean, not about you being ill but about leaving early,' Cleo said. 'I would only have cried my eyes out over that jerk Angus and made a total idiot of myself.'

'It didn't matter to me,' Jade said with a grin. 'It meant I got time with Flynn without you lot hanging around!'

'The main thing,' Tansy said, 'is that you're better now. I think I've had my fill of you practically passing out on me, thank you.' Holly's eyes filled with tears. 'Hey, Holly – don't cry, I didn't mean it like that,' Tansy gasped.

'I meant, you're my best mate and well, to be honest, I've been so useless . . .'

'Useless?' Holly sniffed. 'You? Hardly. You never get in a state, you never panic and you always know what to do.'

'Oh, and look how you came up with the scheme for sorting out that cow Melanie,' Tansy added. 'I was in pieces and couldn't think straight. If it hadn't been for you and Cleo, I could totally have wrecked it with Andy.'

'Listen you lot,' Holly burst out. 'The thing is, I'm really scared about going back to school and if I get one of those awful feelings in class, I don't know what I'll do. There – I've said it.'

'If you feel one coming on, tell one of us and we'll look after you,' shrugged Jade. 'It's no big deal. I got loads of panic attacks after Mum and Dad died. Loads.'

'You did? Truly?'

'Sure I did. I'd sweat like mad . . .'

'Yes, that's right.'

'. . . and feel like I was choking and get pins and needles everywhere, and cry my eyes out . . .'

'So it's not just me? I thought I was going crazy.'

'No more than you usually are,' Jade said, grinning. 'Now do you mind if we eat? Only I promised Flynn I'd phone at nine.'

'I thought,' said Cleo, smiling, 'that you were totally off boys.'

'That,' Jade answered, 'was last week. You just have to wait for the right guy to come along.'

'Sadly,' said Holly, 'some of us seem to wait an awfully long time.'

'There's Ben,' Jade pointed out. 'If he's as keen on you as Flynn says he is . . .'

'Who's Ben?' Tansy and Cleo demanded in unison.

'Just a guy.' Holly shrugged. 'I can hardly remember what he looked like. I'm not that interested.'

She glanced at the menu, and then looked at Jade. 'You're sure you gave him the right mobile number? The new one? Only he hasn't called yet.'

Cleo and Tansy burst out laughing.

'That's a relief,' Tansy said with a giggle, nudging Cleo. 'She's better. We've got the real Holly back.'

Also available or forthcoming from Piccadilly Press:

What a Week Omnibus: Books 1-3
Including:
What a Week to Fall in Love
What a Week to Make it Big
What a Week to Break Free

What a Week Omnibus: Books 4-6
Including:
What a Week to Make a Stand
What a Week to Play it Cool
What a Week to Make a Move

Book 7: What a Week to Take a Chance